Ms. Thang & The Connect
2

Tiece

Text Tiece to 42828 for Updates on New Releases, Spoiler Alerts & Announcements

If you're looking for a Publishing Home, Tiece Presents is accepting submissions. Simply send your 1st 3 chapters to: tiece@tmpresents.com

Raheem "Rah" Delgado

"We ought to go over there and kill that pussy ass nigga!" Heavy huffed with menacing eyes. "I knew he was a snake ass bum. To even have thoughts about killing us shouldn't ever cross his mind as good as we've been to him."

"Chill out Cuz, he'll hang himself."

"Oh, as far as I'm concerned, he's already a dead man walking," Heavy acknowledged.

"That's true," I agreed with a nod of my head. I turned off the monitor that Heavy and I had been watching. The interesting show was called *Kirk's House*. Yea, I had hidden cameras installed inside of his home once the nigga started slipping on my bread. I needed to see what the fuck nigga had going on. He had already lied to Smoke about being short once, but this was actually his third time playing with my money. There wouldn't be a fourth. I'd only been lenient because Smoke was our guy and I knew how he felt about his homeboy. But, cut the bullshit; Kirk ass had to go. The only thing that would buy him a little more time was if he did show up with all my paper. However, after hearing how he really felt about us...

"He better start counting his days," Heavy cut in. Clearly, he was more upset than me. I was always the cooler headed one. Heavy was always the one that went from 0 to 1,000 real quick.

"Well, let's start with this. Make sure the dog K-9 that they're betting on loses this evening. I respect my boy Smoke, but his loss simply will come from being a casualty of war. I won't forget how he took up for us."

"Smoke is a real nigga. His homeboy is a pussy, but don't worry about him. I'm about to make a few phone calls. His misery starts tonight."

Heavy left the room, as I sat thinking about what I'd just heard. I could tell Kirk was a weasel, but I didn't think he actually had the guts to say he wanted us gone. What the fuck was he thinking? There was never a nigga I'd let get away with as much shit as I'd let him get away with. So, to keep insulting my intelligence all the while scheming my demise was more than I could take. The more I thought about it, the angrier I got. His lil punk ass could never. Even the niggas he served had him scared at times and he'd have to call Smoke to save his ass. I had to laugh to myself. I couldn't believe the nigga had grown balls that big to let such words fly out his mouth, but I had something for him. He would surely feel my wrath.

"A'ight cuz, it's taken care of," Heavy said upon entering the room. "What's the name of the other dog that K-9 is fighting?"

"Poncho," Heavy responded.

With that, I sent Smoke a text message.

Put your money on Poncho if you're betting tonight. Keep that between me and you. RAH

Poncho? I don't usually go against my better judgement but if you said it, I will. Preciate that. I was just about to place my bet. SMOKE

No problem Fam. RAH

"Who you texting?" Heavy asked.

"Smoke. I just told him to bet on Poncho."

"Why'd you do that? You don't think he'll tell his boy to do the same thing?"

I shook my head. "I doubt it, simply because of what Kirk said about us earlier and it being me that told him to bet on Poncho. You see, K-9 has always brought them luck and nothing but wins. Either way, Kirk ain't gon' go against that, no matter what."

"I heard that," Heavy responded. "That nigga gon' be sick. Not only is he in the hole with you and The Rotts Organization, but he'll also be in the hole with Smoke."

"I don't even know why he got involved with The Rotts. Ain't nothing but a bunch of old heads with money that's a part of their circle. Kirk was way in over his head. They pay top dollar on card games and dog fights. They ride around on Harley Davidson bikes, smoke expensive Cuban cigars, and drink the finest of Whiskey and Cognac. His dumb ass doesn't fit in."

"How did he even become a part of that society?"

"Well, he had to pay a pretty penny, that's for sure. Initiation is usually around forty-thousand or better. I'm sure Kirk paid the better. See, with his parents being known doctors and him already coming from a wealthy family, they probably saw it as a good thing. Bring in a rookie with a decent background and mold him, but what they didn't know is that Kirk's money doesn't come from his parents or being a doctor himself. The nigga is a drug dealer. He hides behind his family's fortune."

"And ours too," Heavy added.

"You got a point, but I'm not exactly sure if they know anything about that. I highly doubt they would've fucked with him on that tip. Anybody that has sense knows what we're about and, trust, they tread lightly in these waters."

"Which is why his pussy ass has to be another example of why we don't play. I'm thinking you should call another emergency meeting and let me smoke his ass in front of everybody."

"Nah, we wanna do something different this time. Not so dramatic but something that's definitely felt throughout the team," I responded. "He wasn't going to last long anyway. After talking to his ex and really finding out what type of nigga he was left a bad taste in my mouth. What I respected the most though was shawty keeping it real with me. She could've danced around it, avoided it, or shot me a bunch of lies. Yet, she told me everything, including the parts about him abusing her in every which way possible."

"Damn, so it was true?"

"I heard it from her own mouth," I told him.

"I knew Tam was telling the truth. I didn't see a reason why she would lie, but just to know that he really did those things tells us a lot about that nigga. We might have a few bodies on our hands, but they're all niggas. We were taught to never hit a woman and that—"

"Women and kids are not to be touched or used as collateral damages—"

"Or casualties of war," Heavy added.

"Facts. So, to have somebody that close in our circle that's as fucked up in the head as he is has got to go. If that nigga did show up with all my money, he'd still have to go."

"I know right," Heavy agreed. "That nigga must have mommy and daddy issues. If you look at him, you wouldn't even think he's like that. However, I've always known something was a lil off about him. Plus, he likes to floss a lot like he can compete with us. Anytime we're out clubbing, and he shows up, he always gotta draw attention our way by throwing money at the bitches and shit."

I laughed because it never failed. I don't know what Kirk be trying to prove, but that ain't it.

"So, what's up with you, Nova? She seems like chill people."

"She is. I'm digging her, but you know how I am. I'm not getting involved with nan nother woman until I know she's fully down with me and what I have going on. She needs to know about the business and how I get down. She gotta be a rider and down for whatever. Honestly, I don't think lil Ms. Nova is ready for that. She's too prissy and spoiled. I don't think she can hang."

"I thought the conversation went good though."

"Definitely good conversation and she earned a lot of respect from me. But, putting in the footwork? I don't think she's ready for what comes along with being my woman. Nobody has been able to hang yet."

"Ginger almost made the cut," Heavy chimed in, as I shot him the side-eye.

"Almost wasn't good enough. Hell, she was cold with it. She left a nigga while I was sleep, leaving behind a letter that was supposed to make me feel better."

"Well, at least she was honest. Walking in on you killing a man scared her shitless."

"Which is my point. I need a woman that can handle what I do. I never intended on her seeing me kill a man, but the way she screamed out when she entered the room told me that she wasn't fit to be the woman by my side, anyway. Plus, her complaining all the time had run its course." I said, immediately followed by a scowl on my face. "My nigga, did you fart?"

Heavy bust out laughing. "Damn Cuz, that damn pulled pork sandwich got my stomach fucked up. That's why I don't eat pork."

"I tell you to stay away from that unhealthy shit anyway, especially if it got your insides smelling like that." I shook my head.

Heavy laughed. "I gotta shit. I'll be back."

"Please go," I insisted with a slight chuckle. "Your sour ass," I uttered while pulling out my cell phone, along with a joint that I'd rolled while watching *Kirk's House*. All this talk about Ms. Thang had me wanting to call her.

I knew she was going to be surprised, because we never exchanged numbers, but I'd had her contact information ever since that night in the club. I fired up the joint while anticipating the sound of her soft voice.

On the first ring, she answered, "Hello," in a sweet, innocent tone.

"May I speak with Ms. Thang?"

"This is she. Who am I talking to?"

"Who would you like to be talking to?"

"Well, um." I could imagine her smile through the phone. "This handsome guy I know of. He's someone I just recently was shootin' the shit."

"Oh yea? And who might that chans nèg be?" I asked, already figuring that I was the lucky guy she was talking about.

"Well, um, he's fluent in both Spanish and Haitian Creole but loves Asian dishes," she said.

At that point, I knew she'd caught on to my voice and my lingo. Shawty had me kind of blushing.

"He has good hair and baby edges I wish I still had. Not to mention, this nigga is fine, fine," she acknowledged with a cute giggle.

"Ha," I uttered with a slight chuckle back. "Oh, so you trippin', trippin'."

"Nah, I'm serious, serious."

I grinned as I felt myself liking this woman more and more. It felt weird to be attracted to somebody this fast and especially in such an unexpected way.

With me on pause, which was unusual, she laughed out loud. "Hey Raheem. It's good to hear your voice."

I wanted to say the same, but I kept it G. "That's wassup. What you doing tonight?"

"Planning some things to get back on my feet," she responded, as my phone beeped. I glanced at the caller ID screen. It was Smoke calling.

"Hey Hermosa, hold please."

"Okay," she said, as I clicked over.

"Wassup Bruh?"

"I appreciate that win Bruh," Smoke said.

"No problem Fam."

"We'll chop it up later."

"Fa sho', I'll see you tomorrow," I responded. I knew he wanted to say more, but he was wise for not asking questions.

"A'ight Bruh," Smoke said, as we ended the call. I smiled inside while puffing on the joint. I loved to see a plan fall into place. Kirk was probably shittin' bricks right about now not knowing what to do, and I enjoyed every minute of it.

"I'm back Mamacita. Sorry 'bout that."

"It's cool."

"So, what were you saying before I put you on hold?"

"I was just saying that I'm planning some things to get back on my feet."

"Oh, okay, well, that's wassup. So, you've decided to take charge of your life and what's yours?"

"Absolutely," Nova said back.

I smiled. Shawty was not only listening to me, but she was taking action, something that turned me on about her.

"So, when will I see you again?"

"Soon would be something that I'd like to say, but my schedule is unpredictable. I help run a few businesses, on top of other things. Honestly, I rarely have the time. I'm not very consistent with my actions when it comes to being with a woman."

"True, I understand," she eased in.

"But, who knows? If fate will have it, we'll meet up sooner than later. I trust in His timing," I said.

"Well, I'll be waiting. Take care of yourself and have a good night Mr. Delgado."

"Thanks, and likewise, Ms. Thang," I responded with a smile and then ended our call. Heavy re-entered my man cave with a big smile on his face. I looked over at him. "Either your fat ass about to get some pussy or that was one good ass shit."

Heavy laughed, as I chuckled with a shake of the head. "Good news, K-9 lost the fight."

"I know, Cuz. Smoke already called to thank me."

"You won't believe this part though."

"What?" I pondered with a curious frown. "I was told that Kirk lost it."

"What you mean?"

"He bet with K-9, then started feeling like he was set-up to lose, especially having known Smoke had changed his bet to Poncho. I was also told that he and Smoke had a few words, but only after Kirk pulled his gun out on Leroy."

"K-9's owner?"

"Yea," he responded.

"The nigga is like a loose cannon. I'm surprised them boys didn't murk his ass right there on the spot with that bullshit."

"As always, Smoke saved the day, I'm sure. Nobody wants to fuck with Smoke," Heavy acknowledged.

"That's because he's one of us. We treat the nigga more like family than a worker. That's why Kirk be so in his feelings. I'm sure he's been peeped game too. Real recognize real, that's for sure."

"I heard that," Heavy agreed with a nod of the head. "So, Kirk left with Smoke is the word I got."

"Yea, I'm sure he's probably dropping his ass off. His bitch ass got all kinds of niggas wanting him off the streets now."

"Which means that he's really feeling the heat," Heavy chimed in.

"As he should. He may as well count his days," I said, just as my cell phone rang. I glanced down at the caller ID to see that it was Smoke calling.

"Wassup Bruh?"

"I just dropped Kirk off at his house, but I needed to call you about something."

"I've heard," I told him, just so he could bypass Kirk's erratic behavior at the dog fight and get to what's going on with the nigga right now. I went back to my monitor and turned it on to get a look at *Kirk's House.*

"I don't know what's wrong with him. He's been losing his mind. On the outside, he seems chill as fuck but, on the inside, he's a ticking time bomb. That's my boy and all, but he's becoming unpredictable. It's gotten worse since his girl left him. All he wants to do is drink, talk nonsense, and fuck off his money."

"He has been moving out of character," I responded.

"I know," Smoke cut in. "This is deep. I'd rather just talk with you face to face tomorrow."

"That'll work. Come through earlier, so we can chop it up."

"Gotcha."

"Aye, what was he doing when you dropped him off?" I asked, since I was scanning the cameras and didn't see Kirk in his house.

"He got in his car, drunk as hell, against my better wishes. I mean, hell, he's grown, so I let him go. The last thing I wanna do is hurt the nigga."

"I feel you. Well, 'preciate the heads up. See ya tomorrow."

"A'ight cool," Smoke said, and we ended the call.

"Damn, so the nigga is out of control, huh?" Heavy

asked.

"Sounds like it, but he's not home. I wonder where he's going?"

"No telling."

"I need to make a few phone calls," I said, making sure I stayed a few steps ahead of Kirk.

"Cool, and I'll make a few phone calls as well," Heavy told me.

I wasn't the least bit concerned that Kirk was crazy enough to come here looking for us. He wouldn't get past the front gate, for one. If anything, the nigga was running with what little money he did have on him. I needed to put eyes on the airport too.

Over an hour and a half had passed as I waited to hear word back of Kirk's whereabouts. He still hadn't made it back to his house, which led me to believe that he was now on the run. I mean, if I was him, I would skip town too. Just as I leaned back in my chair to stretch my arms out, Heavy entered the room with his cell phone in his hand.

"You gotta hear this," he told me with a serious expression on his face.

"What now?" I pondered, as Heavy put his phone and speaker and proceeded.

"What did Kirk do to you, Tam?"

"Kirk walked in on me while I was sleep. The nigga was talking crazy. I think we scared each other. I don't believe he remembered that I was renting his place out. Once the thought dawned on him, he started talking

14

reckless and loudly. I promise I ain't never seen him like that before. Long story short, he went in the attic and came back down with a black duffle bag in his hand. So, as I began to tell him that he's not allowed to come in here while I'm renting the place, he grabbed me around my neck and stuck his hand up my gown. I tried to scream, but he aggressively covered my mouth. I honestly thought the nigga was about to rape me. His eyes were black and cold as he stared at me but, within seconds, he stopped. He then told me that he was leaving town, but he wasn't leaving Nova behind."

I frowned with uncertainty. "What he meant by that?"

"I don't know. After that, he left."

"Where is Nova now?" I asked.

"I called her and, when she answered, she said she was fine," Tam responded. "I tried to tell her about Kirk, but she rushed off the phone, saying she would call me right back because her mama was beeping in."

I simply shook my head with a shrug of the shoulders. At least Tam had heard from her.

"What you think I should do? I was so scared. I didn't even think to call the police. What if he comes back to try and kill me?" she frantically asked, as if Kirk's unexpected visit had finally hit her.

"Don't call the police," Heavy told her. "Just sit tight. I'm on the way."

I nodded my head, letting him know to go protect his lady. As a sickening feeling came over me, Kirk showed up on my monitor by entering his house. For some reason, being able to see him made me feel better. Once inside, he went straight into the kitchen, his favorite area of the house. He sat the black duffle bag on the kitchen counter and unzipped it. All I could see was stacks of money in it. From experience, it was about sixty-thousand dollars in it. He owed me all of that and some. As I watched his movements, his cell phone rang. The look on his face was that of confusion or contemplating if he should answer it. I couldn't hear the caller, but I could hear him.

"Hey, wassup?" he answered, followed by a pause and then, "I agree. We have some unfinished business we need to settle. You can come over tonight," he said, now cleaning up the glass and plates off his floor. "I ain't going nowhere until tomorrow." After saying that, he said, "Cool, see you in a lil bit."

Once off the phone, while cleaning up the glass, he started talking to himself. "This has been long overdue. It's past time to settle this." He reached in his kitchen drawer and pulled out a small dropper bottle of liquid. Pulling his gun out the back of his pants, he sat it on the counter next to the small bottle of liquid. From what I could tell, he was ready for war or whatever, but with who? Not knowing what to think at this point, I messaged Nova.

You good mamacita? RAH

Never better ☺ NOVA

Okay, good. RAH

You good Hermoso? NOVA

I smiled a little. She called herself speaking Spanish.

Yea just call me if you need me. RAH

Okay, will do. NOVA

I felt a bit of relief that she had responded and was okay. I didn't want to go into full details about what was going on, but the tone of her text suggested that she was fine. Plus, I was able to keep my third eye on Kirk. As long as she was in a safe place, that's all that mattered.

Kirk would be a distant memory by morning. As I waited patiently, my cell phone rang.

"Yea," I answered.

"Somebody is pulling up," my goon on stand-by said.

"I figured that. Just stay in place. If we're lucky, they may handle the job for us."

"A'ight Boss."

The minute I ended that call, my phone rang again. I glanced down to see that it was Smoke this time.

"Wassup my guy?"

"Have you talked to Nova?"

Instantly, my eye twitched as my stomach turned. I never spoke with Smoke concerning Nova, not in a romantic type of way anyway, so for him to hit me up asking that question took my thoughts from 0 to 100 real quick. "She not long ago messaged me. Why?" I asked back while staring at the monitor.

"She sent her cousin a message and said, if she's not back by morning, to call the police and send them to

Kirk's house."

My eyes widened, as my thoughts instantly went back to our earlier text messages of her taking my advice. "Hold up," I said, just as Kirk's doorbell sounded off. Instantly, Kirk put the gun and the dropper inside the drawer, as I could feel my stomach drop. I stared at the monitor in silence, only hearing Smoke's voice on the other end of the phone.

"You think I should ride out there?"

I was glued to the screen, mouth partly open but no words coming out. Kirk made it to his door and, the minute he opened it, Nova walked in. At that moment, I knew she was walking into a very dangerous situation. If I didn't act fast, her blood would be on my hands and I didn't know If I could live with that.

"Rah, you there?"

I cleared my throat, as the unknown of what would happen next weighed heavily on my heart. "Yea sit tight. I'll call you right back."

Kirk Koban

I should bust this bitch head to the white meat, but I'm gon' let her live long enough for me to get a lil revenge satisfaction from breaking my heart and making me look like a fool. I couldn't even lie; I was still shocked that the Ms. Nova Thang had called wanting to see me. I figured eventually she would be asking for her things back and, luckily, she did. Little did she know, I was getting ready to burn all that shit up before skipping town. However, I had no plans whatsoever of leaving her behind. I smiled, allowing her to enter my house as uneasy thoughts raced through my mind. She must've felt she was walking into a safe zone of us mutually talking and then going our separate ways, but I had other plans for her.

"I'm glad you called," I said with a fake smile on my face.

"Me too," Nova responded. I couldn't help but admire how beautiful she was, even with her hair pulled up in a messy ponytail and wearing a simple pair of cut up jeans and an embroidered *Boss Shit* t-shirt, as she followed me into the kitchen.

"You want something to drink?" I asked, hoping that she'd take me up on my offer.

"Nah, I'm good."

"Come on, you can have one last drink with me," I said, as she scoped out the black duffle bag with all of my money in it.

"Is some of that for me?" she asked in a joking way.

"Hell, you can have the whole bag if you give me another chance," I teased back, while hating that a part of me was very serious if the bitch took me back.

"I didn't come here for that. Well, not the part about us getting back together," she quickly assured me. "I just wanted to get my things and I appreciate you allowing me to get them. Now, if you wanna throw in some cash, that would work too."

I grinned, pouring myself another glass of Grand Marnier. I opened the cabinet, pulled out another glass, and poured a little in that glass too. "Well, I need you to know that I wouldn't keep your things from you. You just never asked to get 'em."

"I needed space Kirk. The last time we saw each other wasn't pleasant at all. You hit me like I was a man."

Technically, that wasn't the last time I saw you. I remembered, as flashes of her in Rah's face at the club flooded my memory. I fought to free my mind of the unpleasant thoughts, so I could continue my quest of bringing her ass down from that high horse she was now sitting on.

"It took two weeks for me to get over that black eye you gave me."

"I know and I'm so sorry for that," I told her. "Til this day, I hated that things went that far. I don't know what got into me."

"Well, I hope you're getting the help you said you needed."

"I am and, honestly, I feel like a changed man," I

lied. "It's good to see you though."

"It's good to see you too," she said while looking around my place. "This kitchen is beautiful."

"It could've been your kitchen had you stayed."

"Yea, well, that didn't work out as I had hoped it would either."

"Things could change. All you gotta do is say the word."

Nova apprehensively smiled. I knew that look, as I predicted what would come out of her mouth next. "Well, um, I really just want to get my clothes and stuff. I didn't wanna stay too long."

"That's why I said to have a drink with me. Shit, I'm leaving town tomorrow anyway. I was thinking it was perfect timing that you called. That way I would get to see you before I left."

Nova frowned. "Where are you going?"

"Somewhere far from here," I responded.

"Does Smoke know you're leaving? Your parents?"

"Yea," I lied again. "I just think it's time for a change."

"Oh wow," she said like she was surprised. "I didn't think I'd be coming over for you to tell me that."

"Well, now you know," I responded while pushing the glass of alcohol her way.

"I guess I can have a sip or two since you put it that way."

I smiled. "Cool," I told her. All I needed her to do

was start drinking and I'd finish what I should've started before she left me for Rah.

Nova stared at the glass like she was contemplating if she should even go there with me.

"Why are you acting like that? You act like I've put something in your drink. You saw me pour it right out the bottle. Hell, I'm drinking from the same bottle." At that time, I grabbed the bottle of Grand Marnier and drank from it. "See, I'm still standing."

"Yea, barely." She grinned, causing me to chuckle a little.

"I know I've had my share of this bottle tonight. Guess it's coming from the fact that I'll be leaving all of this behind."

"I still can't believe you're just up and leaving. I mean, you have this big house now."

"Yea, but all this house is nothing if I'm not sharing it with the one I love."

Nova looked away, as if she didn't want to look in my eyes.

"I'm serious. So, it seems that I've run my course in this city. I feel it's time to take my talents elsewhere."

"Your talents?" Nova grinned. "Like you're Lebron James or somebody."

"Hell, I might be to some people."

She shrugged her shoulders with a nod of the head. "That's true. You might be," she agreed, now sipping a little from her drink and sitting the glass back down on the countertop. "What do you plan on doing with the house and the condo?"

"Well, this house will go up for rent. The condo is still mine, but I definitely have to take care of some of paperwork on it. I should've updated that a couple of months ago, but it's never too late."

"I understand," Nova said with the look of impatience in her eyes.

"Well, let's take this party upstairs, so you can gather your things because I hope you know I wasn't going to pack up all that shit by myself."

Nova laughed a little. For some reason, it made me smile to see her laugh. I missed that part of her. I missed her, which was the main reason why I could never leave her behind. "Grab some of those boxes out of the pantry and I'll get some trash bags, so we can get this over with. I know you must be getting back soon. Probably got your girls on standby just in case. Am I right?"

Nova looked over at me with nervous eyes. At that point, I knew I was right, but she smoothly answered back. "Now, why would I do that? I trust that you'll do the right thing."

"I will," I responded. She just didn't know what the right thing was that I had planned for her ass. "So, are you getting the boxes or what?"

"Yea," she said, now walking towards the pantry. As she entered the pantry, I called out.

"You need some help?"

"Nah, I got it," she responded. Just that quickly, I had opened the drawer and instantly added a tasteless powder substance of *special K* in her drink. Special K was a drug best known as Ketamine and used to sedate and incapacitate their victims and, tonight, Nova was my victim. Surely, this would have her ass unconscious; then, I could take full advantage of her. I didn't know if I wanted to seduce her in the worst way, exploit her to a point that she'd never want to come out again, or just kill the bitch and get it over with. Whatever I decided to do, it wouldn't be pretty. As she appeared from the pantry with cardboard boxes in her hand, I smiled at her.

"Here, get your drink. I'll carry those for you. You got all kinds of shit upstairs," I joked, hoping to loosen her up a little in trusting me more.

"Thanks," Nova said as she handed me the boxes and grabbed her drink. I picked up the bottle of liquor and proceeded to take this show up the stairs. Already buzzed and wobbly myself, I tried to hold my composure. However, I knew Nova had known me long enough to know that, clearly, I was already wasted. Maybe it could've been an assumption that I was somewhat weakened in this state, so she vicariously followed me, not knowing what was in store for her ass.

Once inside the bedroom, Nova stopped as if she was taking in the beautiful view of what could've been hers. She sat her drink over on the dresser, as she reached for a box out of my hand and proceeded to unfold it.

"You got some tape?" she questioned.

"Yea," I said, reaching in one of the drawers and grabbing the tape so she could put the box together. After about fifteen minutes, we had put about ten boxes together. She grabbed one of the boxes and headed towards the huge walk-in closet. This was actually her first time seeing all this shit that I'd had put up for her.

"Wow," she said with a surprised look on her face. "You have everything put up so neatly in here. I thought you would've left all of my stuff boxed up."

"For what? I still had high hopes for us," I said, as I stood back and watched her. A part of her could tell that I wasn't such a bad guy after all.

"This is nice. I hate to pack it all up."

"Well, it's all yours, so do what you gotta do. I totally understand. I know you leaving is all my fault and I truly apologize for my behavior. I never meant to hurt you in this way," I responded. Was I really feeling the words that I'd just said? HELL NAWL, but she ain't need to know that.

Nova glanced back over her shoulder at me. She softly smiled. "It's nice to see you in this element. Again, I appreciate you allowing me to get my things."

It was obvious that she wasn't going to break, and it was nothing that I could do to help change her mind. At this point, I was already knee deep in shit that I was going to drown in if I didn't get the fuck outta here. I had people gunning for me. I knew it. I owed Rah lots of money. I was in debt with the Rotts Organization. I had new enemies from pulling out my gun at the dog fight. Like, shit was bad for me now. So bad, I didn't know if I was coming or going. The only good thing that had come out of this was my mom calling to tell me that she and my dad were going to give me the house if I just showed them that I could get my shit together. Man, it all sounded good but, after I deal with Nova, any chance of having a decent life here would be out of the question. The only thing I could do was leave town and get as far away as possible and hope to start over someplace else. I already had an ID with a new name, social and birth certificate that I'd gotten months ago. This plan was already in the making. I just didn't know I'd have to use it so soon.

After Nova had packed a few boxes, she seemed tired as hell as she plopped down on the side of the bed. I took that as my queue to sit down beside her.

"I hate we're going our separate ways. I still love you," I told her.

"I still have love for you too, but I just want to move on," she responded back.

"Are you seeing someone new?"

"No, but I don't plan on just sitting around not doing nothing forever."

"What's that supposed to mean?" I asked, trying not to get upset.

"It means that I do plan on having a life after us," she said, now standing to her feet. "I gotta get these boxes in my car."

"I know, but can't we just talk about this. You know I'm leaving tomorrow. I don't wanna end things this way. I want us to at least be on good terms with each other."

"I believe we are on good terms being that I'm here and I came alone," she said.

"Yea, but you're acting all uptight and shit. Have a toast with me."

"It's not that at all," she said, heading back into the

closet.

"Well, what is it? I believe you have a new nigga on your arm."

"Why would you think that? Oh, well maybe because you're out here in these streets talking salty about me?"

I frowned. "Talking salty about you?"

"Yea, you heard me. But, look, I didn't come here for that. I just wanna pack and leave."

"Fine, pack and leave. You don't have to drink with me even if it's the last time we're in the same room together. You couldn't even have a toast to the good and putting the bad in the past. You just wanna pack and leave like we never had nothing, like we were nothing. That hurts," I said with tears in my eyes. A part of me did feel bad, but the tears was just a means to make her feel even worse about the situation if she had any kind of heart left for me.

"Damn, let's have a toast and, then I'm leaving. I'll get what I can fit in my car and come back tomorrow with Yaz and Tam to get the rest of this stuff."

"That's fine with me," I said as I watched her pick up her glass. "So, are we going to toast to what we had and to moving on?"

"Sure, a toast to moving on to bigger and better. I wish you nothing but the best in whatever you have going on after us," she said.

"Cheers to that," I said, but I really didn't give a damn about her speech. She could take that shit and shove it up her sweet lil plump ass. "A toast to the good life," I added, holding up the bottle since I didn't have a glass. We clinked the bottle and glass together; then, we both took a shot. She actually drank all of it to my surprise, as a big smile appeared on my face. There was no way she would make it back to her family tonight. I was going to make sure of that. A few minutes passed of us talking about me moving far away, and then I could see that she'd grown tired of the conversation.

"So, well, I'm gonna get on outta here," she said, grabbing one of the boxes. "I'll come back with my help to get the rest."

"Okay, I'll help you," I told her, stacking two boxes on top of each other. "I'll follow you." As we made our way down the stairs, I could tell the drink was already kicking in. She seemed to stumble a bit. "You a'ight?"

Nova didn't respond but, the minute she reached the first floor, she swiftly dropped the box and turned to me. "What have you done?" she asked, seemingly unbalanced a bit.

"Nothing," I said, trying not to laugh at her gullible ass. "OH SHIT!" I let out, as Nova pulled a subcompact 9mm pistol out of her pocket.

"Nigga what did you do to me? What was in that drink?"

"Nothing," I said again, as I tried to move around her. Being that she was a little discombobulated this task should've been easy, but Nova was definitely keeping up.

"I should've shot your ass the minute I walked in here and took everything that you owed me!" she slurred.

"Oh, is that how you feel?" I asked, feeling really irritated that this bitch would have the nerve to come in my house with a gun like she was about that life.

"Damn right, that's how I feel. You've been nothing but a bitch ass nigga to me. You used and abused me and, now, it's over."

"Nah, looks like it's over for you." I grinned.

POP!

"OH FUCK!" I yelled out, touching all over my body. "Bitch, you pull that trigger one more time, you better make it count!" I shouted, but the adrenaline pumping through my body now was telling me that I had to get that gun out of her hand. As I charged towards her, the gun fell to the floor and so did she. She could barely move as I stood over her, thinking what I should do to this bitch. I could easily kill her and say it was self-defense. As I reached for her gun, since mine was still inside the kitchen drawer, my doorbell rang.

"Who the fuck is that? I know this bitch ain't have her people waiting outside for me," I whispered to myself. My cell phone started blowing up. I reached in my pocket to see that it was Smoke calling me. I hesitated on answering but answered anyway, as my doorbell continued to ring.

"Wassup?" I said, trying to sound as calm as possible.

"Come to the door," he told me. "I got the rest of the money you need to pay Rah."

I stood in silence as I looked down at Nova's lifeless body. I knew without a doubt that Smoke had seen

Nova's car parked out front so, immediately, I didn't know what to think.

"Man, I see Nova's car out here. So, you finally talked her into giving you another chance?" Smoke grinned. "I know you probably in there tryna make up. So, just come get this money and I'll be on my way."

"Damn Bruh, that means a lot. I know I owe you and I got you as soon as I get back on my feet," I finally responded, but his bitch ass owed me all that money anyway from taking Underwood, instead of telling Rah that I should hold down that spot. Luckily, he had said that stuff about Nova too, or I would've left his ass standing outside. But, as long as he didn't have any plans to come in my house, we were good. I'd get his money and still skip town on them nigga's. I wasn't playing around. I could start all over and wreak havoc in another city. I glanced down at Nova. "Bitch, I'll deal with you when I come back."

I hastily made my way to the front door and, the minute, I opened it...

BOW!

2

Nova Thang

The sound of the phone ringing woke me out of my sleep. I opened my eyes, slowly trying to stretch my arms out while looking up at the ceiling. I could still hear the phone ringing in the background but couldn't bring myself to answer it. It was like I'd been in a deep slumber and unconsciously unable to move like I wanted to. As I sat up in the bed, my eyes widened, not really remembering what had happened. I had a pounding headache as I tried to focus in on my surroundings.

"Where the hell am I?" I whispered, crawling out of bed to stand up but still feeling groggy as hell. I looked at my attire, noticing that I still had on the same clothes as the day before. As I composed myself, somewhat reliving a little of what had happened before I blanked out, I realized where the fuck I was. Quickly, I reached in my pocket looking for the 9mm I had taken out of my father's lock box. Not only didn't I have a clue as to where the gun was, but I also didn't know where Kirk was either. Trying not to panic, I walked over to the closet and opened the double doors. The closet was empty, but my stomach was full of uneasy flutters that had me on the verge of throwing up.

"Kiiirk?!" I called out as I scanned the bedroom

again. I needed to know where his ass was at. As I started to walk towards the room door, I was startled by my cell phone ringing again. I turned to see that it was on the nightstand by the bed. "Weird," I said to myself, making a U-turn to get it. I wasted no time answering once seeing that it was Yaz calling.

"Yaz," I whispered in the phone.

"Novaaaa! Where the hell are you?!"

"What? Huh?" I asked as I glanced around the bedroom. Yaz was on the phone, but it sounded like she was nearby.

"Yaz," I said in the phone again, as I headed out of the bedroom.

"Nova, thank God!" Yaz let out in a relieved breath. "Where are you?"

"I'm still at Kirk's house."

"I know. Your car is out front, and Tam and I are downstairs in this big ass house."

"Downstairs?!" I asked, as I sped down the hallway and ran straight down the stairs. I was so happy to see Yaz and Tam standing there. I ran straight into their arms.

"Girl, we were worried sick about you. I had tried calling you several times through the night, but Smoke called and told me that you were fine and not to worry. Everything was under control and that he wasn't going to let anything happen to you."

"Huh?!" I pondered with a frown on my face. "So, Smoke knew I was here?"

"Apparently," Yaz said, as Tam cut in.

"I even had called Heavy to find out if you and Rah had talked."

"What?!" I asked again. Everything was still somewhat fuzzy as I tried to gather my thoughts as to what had happened.

"Yea, because Kirk tried me last night."

I frowned. "Tried you how?"

"Yea, he showed up at the condo, acting crazy and talking reckless. The nigga pinned me against the wall and stuck his hand up my slip."

"He did what?!" I asked again as I looked around the house, still not seeing any sign of his presence.

"I thought he was going to rape me but, just as quickly as he came, he left. However, the look in his eyes scared the shit out of me. Plus, he was rambling some shit about you not being left behind."

"Me not being left behind?" I pondered. "This is all so strange because he did mention that he was leaving town tomorrow. He said that he was making a fresh start —"

"And, what happened after that?" Tam pondered.

"I don't know. I can only remember packing boxes and then having a toast with him," I said, as certain parts of the night started to come back to me. "He put something in my drink."

"What?" Yaz pondered with a clueless expression.

"He spiked my drink because I remember toasting

with him and then coming down the stairs. I felt faint and kind of sick to my stomach, so I shot at him."

"You did what?!" Tam asked aloud.

"I had taken daddy's gun and I shot at him when I realized that he had spiked my drink."

"Damn, did you kill him?" Yaz asked.

"I don't see no blood," Tam cut in. "Did you hit or miss?"

"I don't know. I don't remember nothing else after that," I said while holding my head. "I feel dizzy."

"Come, let's go in the kitchen so you can get some water," Tam urged.

"I just wanna get out of here," I said as I wobbled a little.

"Wooah, you alright?" Yaz asked. "I think Tam is right. Clearly, Kirk ain't here and you need water. No telling what that nigga spiked your drink with." Yaz pulled me into the kitchen, as Tam wandered about.

"Where is Kirk?" Tam asked. "I have a funny feeling about this. I don't want that nigga jumping out the closet and scaring the shit out of us."

"At this point, he might try to kill us," I said.

"Something is off. I have a bad feeling," Tam said, as Yaz fixed me a glass of water.

"Here, drink this and then we can gather your things and leave."

Tam walked to the back door, as she opened it and walked out on the patio. "Kirk's car is parked in the back yard."

"What?" I pondered, as I walked out to join her. I saw Kirk's car but still no Kirk.

"You don't think you killed him, do you?"

"I don't think so. I can't even remember nothing but shooting at him."

"Tam, where are you going?" I asked.

"I'm going to check his car," she said, walking down the patio steps and out to Kirk's Charger. "He's not in here."

"Go figure," Yaz uttered as something frightened her, causing me to jump in my skin.

"What?!" I asked, looking behind me.

"Something just scared me."

"Something like what?" I asked, trying to see if Kirk had reared his ugly head.

"I don't know. I just caught chills up and down my spine."

No sooner than she could get that out of her mouth, a loud piercing scream startled us both, as we ran down the patio steps to see Tam pointing towards the lake.

"Is that Kirk?" Yaz asked in a shaken tone.

I stood stiff as a board, heart pounding damn near out of my chest as I stared out at a lifeless body floating in the lake.

"Whoever that is, they're dead," Tam finally said, breaking the eerie silence that had snuck up on us.

"We need to call the police!" I frantically said, as I pulled out my cell phone.

"No, we might not need to do that. Let's think first," Tam urged. The minute we stepped foot in the house, a burner phone sitting on the countertop began to ring. I looked at Yaz and Tam as they both stared back at me.

"Whose phone?" Tam asked.

"I have no clue," I responded back.

"Well, don't just stand there, answer it," Yaz desperately demanded.

I nervously picked up the burner phone as my hands trembled immensely; I flipped it open to answer it. "Hello," I apprehensively said.

"Listen to everything I tell you and do exactly as I say."

Page Break

3

Raheem "Rah" Delgado

"Don't call the police, at least not right now," I said as I watched a shaken Nova on the monitor pacing the floor back and forth.

"Raheem?"

"Listen," I told her. "I need you to calm down."

"I can't. I don't know how," she responded, as Yaz stood by in silence and Tam stood staring Nova in the face.

"You have to calm down long enough to listen to what I'm about to tell you."

"Okay," she softly said.

"I need y'all to put your boxes of things in the cars, take the burner phone that you're talking on and put it inside of your glove box until you see me, and make up the bed that you woke up in. I need the house to look like y'all were only there to pack up your things and leave. However, the other two wanted to check out the rest of the house and upon going outside on the patio they   discovered–"

"The body," Nova nervously finished.

"Yes, the body," I acknowledged.

"Is that Kirk?" Nova asked me.

"Once you've cleaned up the scene, only doing as I ask, call the police," I said, ignoring her question. "They will come through and investigate the scene, thoroughly examining y'all's demeanors, and likely look into your phone records. Tell them that you spoke with Kirk last night about getting your things back. You came over, started packing up some things, and realized that it was more than you thought. So, you returned with your girls to finish packing this morning. Everything was fine when you were there, but you could tell that he was pre-occupied and wasted. You have no clue as to why but be clear on the part that he was very drunk. You left and returned to an empty house. Meaning, he was not there, but the door was unlocked. Not that it was unusual because he did tell you to let yourself in."

"Okay," she responded.

"You okay?"

"No."

"I know," I responded, feeling somewhat bad for her and the situation, but I couldn't let it show. "Now, do as I say," I insisted and ended the call. I looked over at Heavy with a shake of the head. "FUCK!!" I let out, as I glanced back at my first cousin Jose and, then, back at the monitor. "This shit could've gone a lot smoother had you been equipped."

"I know Rah but, damn, it ain't my fault," Jose said, as he looked over at Heavy with the look of regret in his eyes.

"Don't look at me like that. You know you supposed to carry two phones on you at all times. Your work phone and your personal phone," he added.

"What if something would've happened to Nova? I would've had to rough you up behind that shit," Heavy said, knowing that's what I would've wanted him to do.

"I know, and I'm sorry about that Cuz. I didn't even realize I didn't have my personal phone until my burner phone died. The minute I realized I didn't have the charger to it is when I realized I didn't have my personal phone either. Instantly, I knew it was Keisha's ass. Ever since she caught me cheating, she's been ridin' me like a fucking member of the Feds association. Always snooping and shit, looking for something that's only going to hurt her more. I'm 'bout tired of her ass."

"Yoooo, Keisha is the baby mama from hell. After your first seed, you should've walked away but, nah, you planted five more seeds in the broad. You'll never get rid of her ass," Heavy chimed in. "She ain't nothing but a damn baby making machine."

"She's down for a nigga, too."

"Yea, only down to have babies, so yo' ass can't leave her."

"How you figure?" Jose asked, clearly getting irritated with Heavy's claims about his baby mama.

"That woman knows so much shit about you that you can't leave. Aside all the children she's had by you, she also knows a lot of your business."

"That might be true, but she would never use any of that shit against me," Jose shot back.

I shook my head just listening to this nigga. He's

lucky he's family or no telling how this shit would've played out for him. I couldn't have Nova's blood on my hands. I wouldn't be able to operate like that. In a sense, I felt the need to protect her, especially after hearing that she was taking my advice. I think she could've handled the situation a lot differently but, hey, I guess she thought she was safe from that crazy ass nigga. Luckily, we made it there just in time because no telling what he would've done to her.

"Cuz, no disrespect, but I really need to have a talk with your woman," Heavy said. "She does way too fucking much. She could cause a nigga to lose their life with the way she be moving."

"Keisha ain't gonna listen to you," he responded. "Plus, I don't need you crossing those lines. Stay in yo' lane and leave Keisha to me. She's my problem, not yours. I'll just have to stay on top of things when it comes to her."

"You need to leave that bitch."

Jose shot Heavy the side-eye. I knew shit was about to get real, real fast, so I quickly intervened.

"Ayyyye, don't do that, Heavy. That's his baby mama. On top of that, they're still together. You wouldn't want nobody calling your baby mama's bitches, would you?"

Heavy looked at me like he wanted to get real disrespectful but, clearly, he knew better. "A'ight, I get it. My bad Cuz," he said to Jose.

"Yea, I hear ya," Jose responded. I'd seen that look in his eyes before and he wasn't too pleased with Heavy talking to him like that. Seemingly, he shook it off, already knowing that family comes first. "But, hey, she is a bitch, a fine ass, best of the best pussy, can suck a mean dick ass bitch," Jose joked, causing us to laugh out loud. "Only I can refer to her as that though."

"I feel ya Cuz. My bad again." Heavy grinned. "Anyway, back to these ladies."

"Yea, do you think they'll fold?" Jose pondered.

"I guess we'll find out," I said, feeling relieved that Tam had done as she was asked which led to everything going as planned."

"My girl came through for us," Heavy acknowledged.

"I agree. You were able to get her to pick up Yaz and go to Kirk's house. She knew to walk in and ask questions about Kirk's whereabouts. She led them into the kitchen and then went out back like you told her to do."

"She didn't know a body was in the lake, but I'm sure she knew that's what I was leading her up to once it was spotted," Heavy added.

"She also knew not to wait on that phone call before they made any moves, which was why she stopped Nova from calling the police. She might be a keeper Cuz," I said with an approving nod of the head.

"She's passing these tests back to back," Heavy responded with a smile.

"So, that should tell you something."

"It tells me a lot," Heavy said, just as my cell phone rang.

"Wassup?" I answered.

"Smoke is here. Should I let him in?" The front gate guard asked.

"Let him in," I answered. "Send him to the cave."

"Gotcha boss."

I looked over at Heavy and Jose. "Smoke has made it here." I looked back at the monitor to see what the ladies were up to, as things were now settling in and feelings were all over the place. I didn't want Smoke to see this just yet, so I turned it off.

"Damn, I ain't gon' lie. I already feel bad for my homey."

"I know right," Jose agreed, as he dropped his head.

Nobody really cared about what had taken place, but we all had a soft spot for a real nigga and Smoke was indeed a real nigga.

"Does he know anything?" Jose asked.

"No more than me telling him to make that phone call to Kirk. After that, I told him to come here," I said, looking at my Rolex timepiece. "And, as always, he's right on time."

"How do you think he's going to feel about what happened?" Heavy asked.

"Knowing Smoke, he'll need us to respect his space, but also to show him love in our brotherly way. After all, he's one of us."

"You're right," Jose nodded in agreeance.

"Are you going to tell him everything today?"

"I think I should. In light of the situation and after speaking with Father, he feels it's only right to be honest and to help him get through a time like this."

"This ought to be interesting," Jose chimed in.

"Do you want us to stick around for this?" Heavy asked.

"Yea, y'all are just as much a part of this as me. Plus, he needs to know that we're here for him no matter what."

"I agree." Jose nodded.

In less than five minutes, Smoke was tapping on the door. "Come in!" I called out. The look on his face already told me that he knew exactly what he was walking into. Well, some of it.

"Wassup Fam," he said, giving all of us dap. Normally, he'd sit down and make himself at home but, this time, he was still standing like he was looking for answers.

"You good?" I asked.

"I don't know yet," he responded. "I just wanna know what happened."

Clearly, he wasn't wasting any time, so I guess I'd just have to get right to it.

"We did it," I said. "We didn't have a choice. The nigga was unraveling. Had we not moved when we did, no telling what would've happened. I really believe he would've killed Nova, especially after she pulled a gun out on him."

"She what?" Smoke asked with a clueless expression.

"Yea, Bruh, she shot at him too," Heavy added.

"I've never known Nova to be that kind of person. What did he do?"

"Before she pulled the gun on him, he had drugged her when she wasn't looking," Heavy revealed, as I sat back just analyzing Smoke's behavior. "He had also planned on leaving town and taking what little money he did have. He had even revealed some of his plans to Nova but, like Tam was saying, he didn't plan on leaving her behind. He'd made that clear a few times."

"Damn," Smoke said with a disappointed shake of the head. "I knew he was a little off his rocker, but I didn't know it had gotten that bad."

"Jealousy is a silent killer and, from the looks of things, he was mad jealous of you too, Fam," Heavy told him. "He had become a liability and, therefore, we had to get rid of him."

Smoke finally made his way to the couch as he sat down. The look of loneliness and despair had taken over. He was indeed hurt behind losing one of his closest allies, but it had to be done. Kirk was an enemy to us all and, if he had lived, we would have regretted it.

"So, he's gone? Kirk is dead?" Smoke asked, with glossy eyes.

"Yes, he's dead," I answered. I could tell that it was taking everything in Smoke not to cry and, as I knew it, he held up like a G, but his heart was torn with just the thoughts of knowing that what I'd just said was the truth. "There's more."

"What?" Smoke pondered with curious eyes.

"Yaz, Nova and Tam are at his house and probably talking with the police now."

"That would explain why she wasn't answering her phone when I called her not long ago," he uttered. "Are they okay?"

"About as okay as they'll get," Heavy responded.

"I knew Kirk would have to pay the price for his evil ways. I just hate it had to happen like it did. I can't say he didn't deserve it, but a part of me wish he had taken a different route in his actions."

"I knew he wasn't shit back when I'd heard he fucked my lady."

My eyes widened. "He fucked Keisha?"

"He did that, and the only thing saved him was his connection to you and your connection to us. However, I knew this day would come. It was just a matter of time. I was only waiting for the nigga to hang himself."

"Damn Cuz, you never told us that," Heavy said.

"I didn't say nothing because it would make my lady look bad. Y'all already don't care for her, but she was vulnerable after finding out about me cheating. I fucked her best friend and, well, she wanted payback. He was just the grimy ass nigga to run to."

"Wow," Heavy uttered. "Shawty is raw with it."

"Tell me about it," I said under my breath. Cuz had his hands full with that one.

"So, why didn't you deal with him back

then?" Smoke asked.

"Because Keisha stuck with her story saying that nothing ever happened between them. However, I'd gotten solid word from a reliable source that it had. Plus, I knew her reasons behind it. She just knew I'd break her fucking neck if she had told me the truth. She's lucky my kids are more important to me than she is. I don't want them growing up without their parents."

I apprehensively took in a deep breath and then released it. "Damn, I almost hate to tell you that it's more."

"More Bruh? You gotta be kidding me. I already feel like I'm in a dream that I'm begging to wake up from."

"Well, put yo' seatbelt on for this shit," Heavy chimed in, as he stood back and watched me hand Smoke a picture.

Smoke held the picture in his hand, studying it over. His head tilted to the side, as if he was thinking, seriously thinking.

"You a'ight Bruh?" I pondered.

Smoke shook his head, as he held the picture closer to his face like he was examining every detail in it. "Who is this man?" he eagerly asked.

I looked at Heavy and then over at Jose. They were anxiously waiting for me to answer him. It was already so much going on; it was almost unbelievable. Not that I hadn't gone through the storms and back or had dealt with things on deeper levels, but this one was personal. Those were the ones that always got to me.

After taking a lil time to feel out how I would reveal such secrets, I realized it was either now or never.

"The man in the picture is our Uncle, and well… he's your Father."

Silence seeped in the room as we all looked at each other, waiting for Smoke to say something. He continued eyeing the picture, clearly at a loss of words.

Smoke shook his head, confused as ever. "I don't understand. How could this man be my father?"

"He is. My father told us, and he says that my uncle told him years ago that you were his."

"Which makes you our cousin," Jose cut in with a smile.

"Your uncle told your father that I was his child? None of this makes sense. My father's name is Jerry Harris."

"He's not your biological father though. Pablo Delgado is your biological father," I told him with a serious expression. Smoke eyed the photo again. In all honesty, he favored our uncle a lot. Hell, he even favored us, which would've explained when we started hanging out, that women would say we all looked alike. However, back then, I didn't know, but now it made sense.

"If this is true, how come I'm just finding out?" he asked while scratching his head. "I've been kicking it with y'all for years. Nobody said nothing."

"My father and my uncles have always known this. Unfortunately, it was top secret and we weren't privy to none of this until you started working with us. It wasn't until you went against Kirk for our best interest that he decided to fill me in. He looked at it as destiny and a sign from the heavens that it was time for you to know. So, that's when we were told to tell you."

"Yoooo, this craaaazy. Real crazy," Smoke let out, still in disbelief. "Your dead uncle is my father?"

"Yes and, if you don't believe us, ask your mom," I told him. "From what we're told, she and Uncle Pablo were lovers some thirty years ago. They were linked for years, until my uncle got with Aunt Ruby. Your mom then got with that guy Jerry and had a baby. Jerry was said to be your father, but it wasn't until years later when Uncle Pablo asked for a paternity test—"

"But what made him ask for that after years had gone by?"

"Well, he'd known about Jerry abusing your mom and wanted to step in after seeing you playing outside one day. He told my father then that he knew you were his. He could feel it in his soul, and you looked just like him. True enough, Jerry was some mixed guy, which was probably how your mom fooled him like you were his, but he doesn't have the Mexican bloodline that runs through our veins. Your mom knew this; she just kept it a secret. It could've been that Jerry would've killed her if he had found out, but Uncle knew better."

"So, was a test ever taken?"

"Not to my knowledge but everyone knows. I mean, look at you. Plus, my uncle wouldn't lie about something like that if he knew it to be true. You look like one of us. I know you know that Jerry ain't your father. Just think about it," I told him. I could tell his head was spinning and his thoughts were likely all over the place. Without entertaining the subject any longer, he looked at us with a serious stare, followed by a shake of the head.

"I gotta go. I'll holla at y'all later," he said and abruptly left.

4

Rashad "Smoke" Rivers

The minute I walked in my crib, I headed straight for the Hennessy that was sitting on my kitchen counter. I opened the bottle and poured a cup full of it. After the news I'd just gotten, I didn't know if I was coming or going. The man I'd known as my father, really wasn't my father. I couldn't believe it, but I had no choice. The proof was staring me right in the face every time I looked at the picture of this man that I resembled so much. The only difference was our skin tones and the grade of our hair. I was definitely a little more tanned than he was, and my hair was a lot wavier compared to his being of a silky straight texture. I didn't know why it never dawned on me, but ever since I'd been hanging with Rah and the guys, females always said we looked alike. Even Kirk teased me a time or two, but it went over my head. Jerry was of a mixed race and, at times, I felt I looked more like my mom than him, but now I could see another view of something new. I just couldn't believe that they knew but didn't tell me. I guess it explained why they treated me more like family than anybody else on the outside. It was because of me that Kirk got treated like royalty also in certain situations.

I poured myself a drink and turned it up. My body needed the liquid courage to deal with the shit that was going on in my life. My heart was broken into tiny pieces that were scattered about and would probably take a long time to put back together again. I'd lost my best friend, the one person that I was closest with for many years and to know that he was gone did something deep within my soul. It was hard to fathom that he'd take things so far, as to no regards for his life or his well-being. He knew better than to cross Rah. He knew that things would end up badly for him. He knew that even I couldn't save him this time around. I just didn't know what he was thinking. Just thinking about it tore me up inside. This had to be one of the most unbelievable days of my life.

I pulled out a chair from under the table and sat down. Unpleasant thoughts invaded my mental, as I fought back the tears that were desperately trying to escape my eyes. I drank all of the liquor in one gulp and wasted no time pouring another cup. The only thing I wanted to do was drown my sorrows and hope that the days would go by quickly, so I could try and forget that this ever happened. It was already hard, and it was just the first day. Surviving was a must but living with the guilt of not being able to save Kirk would hunt me forever. As I sat wallowing in my misery, the doorbell rang. I drank from the cup once more, and then sat it on the kitchen table as I headed to the door.

"It's me, Yaz. Open the door, Babe."

I opened the door to the sweetest face there was and, without being able to control my emotions any longer, I fell on my knees, wrapped my arms around her waist and wept like a baby. There was no room to feel humiliated or embarrassed. As a man with a wounded soul, I cried for the best friend that I couldn't save. I cried for the father I never knew. I cried for the pain that had finally grabbed my heart and made me feel again. I was hurt like I'd never been hurt before, and, somehow I knew I had to gather my strength and shake this feeling of guilt that was trying to consume me.

"It's okay, Babe. It's gonna be okay," Yaz assured me, as she held me in her arms.

As time passed, we'd made it back in the crib and was now sitting in the living room. I had finally gotten myself together, as I fired up a joint that I had just finished rolling.

"So, how are you my love?" I asked, as Yaz sat over on the sofa with sadness in her eyes.

"Ironically, I feel bad. I don't really know how to feel about Kirk being dead, but I feel bad for Nova. She's hurt just knowing that he's gone and it's just a sad situation that it had to come down to that."

"I agree," I said.

"I also feel bad for you, too. I know that he was your best friend and business partner. I did everything in my power to hold you up when you were down because I honestly wanted to break myself."

"I appreciate you being here for me," I told her with a slight smile on my face. "Were y'all there when they pulled Kirk out of the lake?"

"Yea, but we didn't see him. We didn't even know for sure that it was him until after we'd made it back to my house and Nova got the call from his mother. It's not like we didn't know it was him, but we didn't want to stick around to get the news while we were there."

"I feel you," I responded.

"Nova was so shaken that the police only asked a few questions and, then, they let us leave."

"So, did she say anything about what had happened while she was there alone with him?"

"She said that she only had stopped by to get her belongings and leave. They had friendly conversation. She did mention that he seemed to have something heavy on his mind, but she wasn't there to figure out what it was. She also told them that he was drunk, very drunk that he could hardly walk without stumbling. She then said that she really just wanted to get her things and leave. She mentioned that they even drank a little with a celebratory toast of them moving their separate ways and that was about it. So, the only reason why we were there that morning was because she had a lot more stuff than she realized, and Kirk gave her permission to return with us to help her pack up the rest of her things."

"So, she really didn't tell the police what really happened?"

"No and luckily, she didn't, because the last thing we wanted was to be suspects in his murder when I know we didn't do it."

"You're right, nobody wants that type of smoke."

"But, we do know that he spiked her drink and would've tried to hurt her or worse had God not intervened on his devious, unpredictable plans."

"Damn, I'm still lost for words when it comes to that. I can't believe he had taken it that far. All of this is unfathomable."

"But you believe it, right?"

I nodded my head. "I believe it all. The Kirk I'd known for years was a cool dude. He changed into somebody I didn't know. At first, I didn't wanna believe it, but that night he pulled his gun out on me I knew then that he wasn't the same man I'd known before. It's like his attitude got worse and it didn't help after Nova had left. On the outside, it was like he had all his shit together but, on the inside, he was falling apart."

"So, do you really know who did that to him?" she asked but, deep down, I figured she knew. She was just trying to feel me out.

"There are some things I'd rather just leave be. Just know it wasn't me."

"I know it wasn't you, Babe. No matter what kind of man he was, you couldn't do that to him. I hate to say this but *assho*—" she said but caught herself, "uh... Kirk may not have deserved to go out that way, but he was asking for this. He couldn't just keep treating people like shit and think he's getting over. He wasn't a very nice guy, not to Nova, me, her parents or not to his parents either. Come to think about it, he did Tam wrong too. He had no business entering her space just because he was renting it out to her. Not to mention, she thought the nigga was going to rape her. He turned out to be a real asshole."

I couldn't do nothing but shake my head in disgust. Kirk really had turned to a monster. Maybe it was best that he was gone. He would've brought all us down with his unpredictable ways and despicable behavior. As I sat consumed in my thoughts, my cell phone rang. I glanced down at the display screen to see that it was Mr.

Koban calling me. For some reason, the nerves in my body began to twitch with uncertainty of what all he had to say. I looked over at Yaz.

"It's Kirk's father."

Yaz hunched her shoulders with curious eyes. "Answer it. They don't know you know he's dead yet."

"You're right." I responded and answered the call. "Mr. Koban, how are you this morning?" The line was silent for a few seconds, as I could tell that he was choked up and couldn't speak. Finally, he cleared his throat.

"Have you heard the news?"

"No sir. What news? Is everything okay?"

"No," he said, as silence snuck back in and, finally, he cleared his throat again. "Kirk is dead."

"Kirk is what?" I responded like I didn't know.

"He's dead Rashad. He's dead."

"No, are you sure?"

"I wish I wasn't making this call right now, but I'm positive. They pulled his body out of the lake behind his house a few hours ago."

"Are you serious? This can't be true."

"I wish it weren't," he said, now crying in the phone. I felt so bad for him. I knew that they would take this hard. It didn't matter that Kirk was the black sheep of the family; the only thing that mattered was that he was their family, a son and a brother that they still loved no matter his transgressions or rude behavior.

"Wow, I'm at a loss of words," I said as the tears

started to fall from my eyes again. I was now sad for them and their loss.

"We are too," Mr. Koban acknowledged. "I'm gonna end this call now because I have to comfort my wife. We haven't even called Vanessa or Phillip yet. I don't even know how to bring myself to telling them. I did just wanna ask you, when was the last time you saw him?"

"I dropped him off at his crib last night after we'd left a dog fight. The last time I saw him, he was getting in his car, but we went separate ways. I really couldn't tell you what happened after that," I answered.

"Thank you, Rashad. I'll call you later this week with details of his memorial. You can come by the house anytime though."

"Thank you, Mr. Koban. I'm so sorry for your loss. He was like a brother to me."

"I know, so it's your loss too. We'll talk later, son."

"Okay," I said and ended the call. I looked over at Yaz as I wiped my tears. "This shit is still unbelievable. It's just hard for me to wrap my brain around it, even though I know he's gone."

"I know," Yaz said, as she walked over to me. She straddled my lap, facing me. "I love you Smoke and, anything you need, I'll be here to provide. I just want you to know that you're not in this alone."

"Thanks Bae, I wholeheartedly believe that," I told her. The look in her eyes was sincere. She had a contagious smile that made me feel good inside. I'd never been with anyone that made me feel this way. She was as down as they came and, without a doubt, I knew she'd ride to the ends of the earth and back with me. As we intimately stared at each other, I couldn't help grabbing her beautiful face, pulling it closer to mine, and kissing her passionately. Just that quickly, I'd gotten a hard-on and was ready to fuck. I desperately needed to take my mind off of the current situation and into something more exhilarating.

She started to kiss me softly on my neck, one of my hot spots and then aggressively pulled my white tee over my head. She wanted me just as bad as I wanted her. As we kissed with such intensity, I somehow slipped off my jogging pants with her still straddling me. Assuming I needed help, she kneeled down on her knees and pulled off my boxer shorts. Now holding my pipe in her hands, she glanced up at me with the sexiest stare ever and began to suck on my dick like a very tasty lollipop. She twirled her tongue around the head, causing my eyes to roll back, as I let out a light groan of pleasure. She began to lick around my shaft as if it were a chocolate ice cream on a cone. She was jacking my dick while sucking and slurping at the same damn time. This shit had me caught up in a world that I wished I could stay in forever. As I felt myself about to erupt from such force of pleasure, she slowly eased off it, but at once straddled me again. This time, sitting on top of my hard cock and riding the waves like a surfboard professional while whispering confessionals in my ear.

"I love you," she softly said. "I love you, Rashad Rivers. I love you."

Daaamn, I mentally thought while feeling her warm juice box wrapped around my python, as if it was never letting go. Her walls were wet and succulent as she bit down on her lip, bouncing up and down, back and forth, slow and fast. I could barely keep up as I palmed her ass cheeks and enjoyed the moment. We kissed like it was the last time our lips would touch each other and, before I knew it, we were both cummin' with ecstasy. Yaz grinned a bit while planting soft kisses on my neck; then, she let out a startled shriek.

"What?!" I questioned, as she jumped up off of me. I looked back, seeing that Beans had just let herself in and was standing there like she was in a state of shock from watching us. "What the fuck?! How long you been in here?"

"I'm sorry," she said, batting her eyes. It was obvious she was trying to erase the thoughts of me fucking Yaz out of her mind. "The door was unlocked and so I just let myself in."

"Obviously," Yaz uttered with a slick roll of the eyes. She grabbed her things and looked at me. "Put your clothes on. I'll be back once I freshen up." As she left the room, Beans looked at me with a bit of sadness in her eyes.

"I only wanted to make sure you were alright. Have you heard?" Beans asked.

"Yes, I've heard," I told her while slipping on my boxer briefs and then my joggers.

"I know that you and Kirk were like brothers. I wanted to stop by and pay my respects in person. You know we all go way back."

"I know," I told her. We had yet to sit down and

have a real conversation about ourselves and the baby, yet now we were having to deal with this. Things in my life had certainly gone from 0 to 100 real quick.

"Are you okay? Well, from the looks of things, I'd say that you're just fine," she mocked, clearly upset about what she had just seen.

"Sorry about that," I said with an irritable shake of the head. I didn't even know why the fuck I was apologizing. Hell, she intruded on my space. I didn't invade hers.

"It's cool. I guess that's what people in love do," she responded. "Look, I just wanted to say that I'm sorry to hear about Kirk and, if you need me, I'll be here."

"Thanks," I said as I caught her staring at my chest with eyes that were turned on by what she was looking at. "You a'ight?" I asked, now grabbing my white tee and putting it on.

"Uh, um yea, I'm fine," she answered and turned to leave. "I'll talk to you later."

"Hold up," I said, stopping her. "I know I have to deal with Kirk's death, but we also have to talk about the baby. He'll be here before we know it and I just wanna make sure that we're on the same page and that everything is good with him and with you."

"I know. Hopefully, we can sit down and talk soon."

"Soon, before he's born, I would hope."

"I'll keep in touch," she said and turned to leave.

I wanted to reach out and hug her. I knew it was a part of her that was hurt about Kirk. She'd known him just as long as she'd known me. For some odd reason, they actually got along with each other. We'd all hang out and shoot the shit from time to time, so I knew it was a part of her that was affected. I was sure it was the part that was more so attached to me. Yet, I couldn't hug her at a time like this, simply because it felt wrong being that I still had Yaz all over me. Beans wouldn't like it and I didn't feel right doing it, so I let her leave.

"You okay?" Yaz asked as she appeared behind me. I turned to her, now consumed with the thoughts that I was so desperately trying to forget.

"Not now, but I will be."

5

Nova Thang

Five days had passed since Kirk's death and the shit was still weighing heavily on my mind. The only comfort I found in his death was knowing that it wasn't mine that everyone was grieving. Kirk was an unstable man and all the signs were there. I just didn't know why it took me so long to leave him. I could've easily fell victim by going over there trying to get my shit back. Although I was fully equipped for the bullshit, I wasn't fully prepared for what he'd done to me. Every moment of just thinking about it, I thanked God. I knew Raheem had something to do with saving me, yet he had yet to say it. I guess as long as I knew, that's all that mattered to him. As I sat dwelling over the last few days, my cell phone rang. An instant smile covered my face the minute I saw it was my Hermoso.

"Hello," I answered.

"Wassup Mamacita. How are you feeling?"

"About the same, but I am better than earlier this week."

"You sound better," he said. "What's your plans for today?"

"Well, I'm getting ready to go to Kirk's parents'

house. His mom called me last night and asked if I'd come over. It's probably because they're laying him to rest tomorrow. I'm not sure, but I guess I'll find out once I get there. I hope they don't think I'm staying around too long. After all, Kirk and I wasn't together for the past couple of months. I'm sure they know that by now."

"What are you doing after that?"

"I'm meeting up with Tam and Yaz at the condo. Tam probably has to move out now, I would think. The house is still in Kirk's parents' name, so the condo probably is too. I don't know. It wasn't like he put me in a lot of his business. All I knew is that we lived good, so I didn't question much else."

"I feel you but, after you link with your girls call me. I would like to see you later."

I smiled hard as hell. I'd been waiting all week to see his handsome face. He just didn't know, but he had just made my entire day. "I'll make sure to call you," I told him, not wanting to sound too desperate.

"A'ight, be safe while you're out."

"I will and thanks," I told him. It was nice to talk to someone that cared about my well-being and wanted to make sure I was good.

"Talk to you soon."

"Sure thing, talk to you soon," I said and ended the call.

I stood up from the couch, as I looked around Yaz's place. I couldn't thank her enough for being there for me. She'd been like a superwoman, making sure I was good, being there for Smoke to make sure he was good, and continually working at the restaurant with my dad on a daily. She was off today but spending time with Smoke, and rightfully so. He was definitely taking it harder as the days went by. Kirk was like a brother to him and, even though he knew this day was coming sooner than later, it was just as much a hard pill to swallow for him as it was for me. As I grabbed my purse to leave, my cell phone rang. I glanced at the display screen to see that it was Yaz calling me.

"Wassup Sis?"

"You left yet?"

"Nah, but I'm about to leave now. I had just grabbed my purse to walk out the door."

"Oh ok. I was gonna come home first since Smoke is getting ready to leave too. But, I'll head on over to Tam's house. Find out as much information as you can while you're over there, Sis. Tam is so paranoid that she'll have to move immediately. But, I told her don't worry, she can live with us until she gets her a place if that happens."

"Oh, I will, don't worry. I need to know what's going on anyway. I don't even wanna attend the service tomorrow, but I don't wanna seem cold-hearted either."

"Don't worry, I'm going to go with you. Smoke said that his mom wanted to ride with him, so that's good. He'll need all the support he can get."

"How is he?" I pondered while walking out to my car.

"He's okay. I haven't seen him cry since the day it happened, but I can tell he's sad. I mean, Kirk was some-body he talked with every day. Eighty percent of their time they spent together. Hitting up the clubs, holding down their territories or just talking shit on the phone. So, I know he misses him. He just doesn't really like to talk about it now. It's like he's trying to suppress those memories in order to move on. But, I keep telling him that it's okay to remember the good times. Just don't let his death consume him."

"Yea, I feel you. I try to forget about a lot of it too, though. So, I can understand how he's feeling. It's just sad that it had to be that way. It's unfortunate, but he was asking for it. If it didn't happen then, it was going to happen sooner than later."

"You're right. It's definitely unfortunate, but I agree," Yaz said, as I was driving over to Kirk's parents' house.

"Well, I'm gonna listen to my music now. Just to clear my thoughts a little and I'll call you back once I leave there."

"Ok, love ya chick."

"Love you too," I responded and ended the call.

Within twenty minutes or so, I was pulling up to the Koban's nice estate. The house was three stories and beautiful. It hadn't been many times that I visited, but they definitely knew of me and that I was Kirk's lady- once upon a time. There were a few cars already here; I assumed family members or close friends that was showing their respect to the family. I parked on the side of the road, just following suit as the other cars that were there. Sitting in the car for a bit, I just needed to get my thoughts together. Finally, I got out, ready to get this over with. As I stepped up to the front door, the beautiful wreath hanging on it was a clear reminder of why I was here.

The door swung open before I could even knock. "Hey Nova," Vanessa said as she greeted me with a hug.

"Hey Vanessa," I said back. "I'm so sorry for your loss."

"It was your loss too," Vanessa responded. I didn't know if she knew that it was over, but clearly the police had to have mentioned that the only reason we'd found Kirk's body in the lake was because I was there packing up my shit.

"Nova!" Mr. Koban called out as he walked over and hugged me. "It's been a long time."

"I know. I'm sorry I didn't come around much."

"It's okay. Kirk didn't come around much either. I just wish he was here now," he said with saddened eyes.

"I know, we all do," I responded. I guess a part of me wanted him here just so none of this would be taking place now. I wish he could've gotten the help he needed, and things would've been fine.

"Come on in the kitchen where my wife is at. She's been waiting on you."

I followed Mr. Koban, passing the family room where a few of their guests were mingling, and into the kitchen where Mrs. Koban and their son Phillip were at. Both were sitting at the kitchen table. Mrs. Koban had a glass of red wine in her hand, and Phillip had a glass of brown liquor in front of him. He looked up at me with the saddest expression ever. His eyes were puffy and red like he'd had a long week. Mrs. Koban looked just fine.

Maybe it was a front being that other people were there too, but she was holding up pretty good from what I could tell.

"Hi Nova. It's so good to see you," she said.

"It's good to see you too," I said, leaning down to hug her. "Hi Phillip."

"Hi Nova. I wish we could've seen each other on different terms, but it's nice to see you again."

"I know and I'm so sorry for y'all's loss. This is a shock to me as well. I've been so out of touch with reality all week."

"I know the feeling," Mrs. Koban said. "Please, have a seat," she told me, pointing at the chair next to her. I sat down, not knowing what to say.

"Have something to drink?"

"Uh, no ma'am," I responded.

"Nonsense. Phillip, pour her a glass of Merlot," she said, as Phillip wasted no time pouring the wine in an empty glass that was already at the table. Guess she had plans of me getting lit with them before I even got here. Luckily, I didn't think they were anything like their Kirk or I would've had second thoughts about drinking anything they offered. "This isn't a special occasion, but it's probably one that we'll never have again, at least not together," she said, staring into my eyes.

"I understand," I said, taking a sip of the wine.

"Kirk's obituary has been drawn up already. We have you in it as *a dear friend.* It had come to my attention that you two had broken up quite some time ago by the police. He never mentioned the split to me, but I still feel like you deserved to be a part of his memorial. I hope you don't mind."

"No ma'am," I said, taking another sip of the wine. I didn't know how to feel about that, but at least she didn't say that I was his girlfriend or his significant other. I had been with the man going on four years, so I guess I didn't mind being acknowledged as his dear friend.

"You will be attending the service tomorrow, right?" Mrs. Koban asked.

"Yes ma'am," I responded, even though I really didn't want to go. However, paying my respect was the least that I could do for her son.

"Okay, thank you. I don't know what type of relationship you and my son had because he rarely came to visit. However, the few times that we met you were very pleasant. You seem like a sweet, intelligent woman and something about you must've made a part of him really happy," she said, pulling out some paperwork that was inside a folder. I didn't even notice it sitting on the table in front of her, but she handed the papers over to me. I frowned as I looked over at her.

"What's this?"

"This is the deed to the condominium that you two were living in. Kirk paid this off last year and put the deed in your name."

My mouth dropped open, as my eyes widened. "He did what?"

"Yes, he put the condo in your name. I don't know what that was about, especially with the two of you

67

going your separate ways, but I couldn't keep this from you. Maybe he intended on changing it back to his name at some point, not expecting what had happened to him. Nevertheless, it must've been meant for you to keep it."

"Wow, you have gotta be kidding me, right?"

"No," she said with a shake of the head.

I looked over the paperwork with fine eyes, making sure I didn't skip a beat and, sure enough, Kirk had left the condo to me. He never mentioned it, never acted like it was even paid for, let alone putting it in my name. That would explain why he said he had paperwork to take care of before he left town. My only thoughts were wondering if he was going to sell it or just take my name off the deed. I didn't know, but I sure as hell wasn't going to say nothing about it.

"I do know that the condo is being rented out at the moment, but she will have to move if you plan on residing there. You can give her a thirty-day notice. This has come as a surprise to even me, so I'll pay the first month's rent and deposit on a new place for the tenant because of the inconvenience of it all. I can personally speak to her about that myself, being that I have her contact information now."

"Wow," was all I could say as I continued looking over the paperwork. I heard what she was saying, but I was too deep in my own world.

"I know the feeling," Phillip finally eased in. "I'm still wondering where he got all that money from to pay it off."

"Phillip, you're a very smart man, so don't start acting dumb now. We both know how Kirk was making his money," Mrs. Koban bluntly stated.

"I guess," Phillip stated, then drinking his wine.

"Did you have any more information for the police?"

"Uh, um, no ma'am," I said, still focused on the deed. It's like I had to pry my eyes off the paper. "I only told them what I knew and that's that I'd come to pack up my things, which I did. He and I packed a few boxes that would fit in my car that night; then, I told him that I'd get my best friend or my cousin to follow me back out that morning to pick up the rest of my things. When we got there, the door was unlocked and I let myself in. I didn't think anything of it because he knew I was coming back. We started packing my things and that's when my best friend walked out back to check out the scenery and spotted—" I cleared my throat, not even wanting to complete the sentence. I could see Mrs. Koban's eyes water up, but she held it in like a G.

"Your best friend is also the woman renting out the condo, right?"

"Yes ma'am," I responded.

"I hate y'all had to be there to see that. I wish I knew what happened to him, but I can only imagine. The autopsy didn't even show any signs of a struggle, if there was fight. He had really high levels of alcohol in his system. So much so, that the police said they were surprised he was still walking around."

"Yea, he was very drunk before I left."

"So, from what they could tell, he had wandered off by the lake, slipped in but bumped his head on the way down and that knocked him unconscious. Being as intoxicated as he was, he couldn't pull himself from the water, therefore he drowned. The only thing that bothers me is knowing about the camera's in that house. Strangely, none of the cameras show anything that entire day, let alone that night when this happened. Ironically, there had been no footage since a week prior to that happening."

"Dang that is strange." I said drinking the wine.

"He was alive when you left there but was dead when you came back that morning, right? So, from what I understand, it happened sometime after you left. I'm just glad that you weren't there too, or this could've been a double drowning," she said. "If it was foul play." I could clearly tell that she felt something was off, so I intervened in hopes of calming her thoughts as much as possible.

"It's unfortunate. But the autopsy did say that he had a lot of alcohol in his system. I even told the police that, because he'd had a lot to drink before I even got there and was still drinking when I left. So, I was thinking that he walked out to the lake to admire the view and get his thoughts together because it was a full moon. I don't know, maybe that's when he fell in," I said, shrugging my shoulders.

"That sounds good," Phillip uttered with a shake of the head.

"The report did say that he had triple the limit of consumption. I wish I knew what my child was going through. He just never cared to share his personal life with me. He expressed his displeasure in the way we raised him, but I feel that his father and I did the best we could."

"You and dad took very good care of us. Kirk was and has always been a different breed, although he has the same bloodline. It's like he had different personalities growing up. One minute he would be cool, the next minute he'd be hot as hell with us. It was like he was missing more than just you and dad."

"It hurts that he grew up, moved out, and got deep in the streets. It's like we didn't teach him anything. We tried. He went to the best schools. I even got him counseling because he was so overly hyper and inattentive. I thought it was something that he'd outgrow but it seemed like it only had gotten worse over time. Did you ever experience any issues out of Kirk, like anger problems or anything of that nature?"

"Well—"

"He's gone now, so don't try to protect him," Phillip said staring me straight in my eyes.

"Well, he definitely had a temper that would go from 0 to 100 real quick. I honestly don't even want to talk about this or think about it. I will say that it was the reason why I decided to leave him for good."

"I figured that much," Mrs. Koban said with sincere eyes. "This is all my fault. Had I paid more attention to him. Had I been honest with myself and my family, all of this could've been prevented."

"Honest with yourself and the family? It's been

way past time for this conversation. Please, just leave the past where it's at," Mr. Koban insisted as he entered the kitchen. "It's too much going on as is."

Mrs. Koban seemed to snap back to her senses as she looked over at her husband. "This is too much."

I looked over at Phillip, who was also looking at him mom with curious eyes. "You okay mom?"

"No," she answered. "But, I will not do this in front of Nova or have this conversation period. It's over and done with," she said, standing up from the table. She leaned down and gave me hug. "It was good seeing you, Nova. I hope to see you tomorrow. I feel tired and worn out. I'm going upstairs to lay down."

"Okay, thanks for inviting me over and giving me this news," I said, holding up the deed to the condo that now belonged to me. "I truly appreciate it because you didn't have to," I told her.

"That's the least I could do for your troubles," she sadly said and walked off.

"Well, I think I'd better be going," I said as I stood up from the table. The only thing I wanted to do was get the hell out of there quick, fast and hurry. Phillip didn't even stand up to walk me out. He seemed preoccupied, and I had no clue what none of that was about.

"Come Darling, I'll walk you out," Mr. Koban said. He walked me to the door. I lightly hugged him and made my way back to my car. It was the strangest of events that had taken place, but I had a whole crib that was now mine. I couldn't be mad at that. It was the only good thing Kirk had done for me and I was going to accept it, whether he intended to leave it that way or not.

6

Tamara "Tam" Newton

"Thanks for bringing us lunch. I do appreciate this," I said while watching Heavy take the Olive Garden entrees out the bag and sitting the food on the table.

"It's the least I could do after the crazy shit that happened last night," he responded.

"Your baby mama was about to get her ass beat but, out of respect for your daughter, I allowed her to show her ass and not say anything back."

"Thank you for that. Shawty knew I was having company before she even showed up to pick up our daughter. I don't know why she was even acting like that."

"So, I'm confused here. She knows that you and her aren't in a relationship, right?"

"Right."

"Well, what's her problem?"

"For one, she knows that nobody has ever come to my house except for my other baby mamas. My other baby mamas are no threat to her. My oldest kids' mom is married and my middle baby mama has moved on as well. We co-parent with no issues whatsoever. Simone doesn't have a nigga in her life except for me and that makes her a bit territorial. On top of that, a new woman was at my house and, even though I told her that I had company, I think it didn't sink in until she'd gotten there and seen you."

"Well, she literally showed her ass. Some parts of the act were rather funny but, when she threatened me, I think she took it to another level."

"Yea, well, you saw what I did after that. She had no business showing off in front of my daughter like that anyway. I don't know what the hell she was thinking."

"I don't want to cross any lines or overstep my boundaries, but when was the last time y'all fucked?"

"Night before last," Heavy responded like it was nothing. His truth irritated the fuck out of me, but I could only respect it.

"So, don't you think that's why she was acting a fool?"

"I'm sure it was but, at the end of the day, we're not together," he said with an unbothered shrug of the shoulders.

"Well, so what am I to you?"

"You're someone that I'm close with. I was drawn in from the moment I laid my eyes on you. Once getting to know you and seeing how you're down for a nigga in such a short period of time definitely has me looking at you in an even brighter light."

"So, but you say all that to say that I'm just someone you're close with?"

Heavy frowned like I'd said the wrong thing. "If I'm saying that we're close, then that should mean something. I'm not close with too many people, men or women. I don't know if you're looking for something deeper but, right now, I'm not ready to just jump in a full-blown relationship."

"Because you can't stop fucking other women," I uttered.

Heavy grinned and brushed that shit off. "How's Nova?"

"She's doing good, I guess."

"Did you hear anything else about having to move?"

"Nah, but Nova went over there today and Yaz told her to ask for me. She and Yaz should be making their way here soon."

"I know I've said it before, but I really appreciate you holding shit down when you were at Kirk's house that morning. Things worked out as planned because of you."

"No problem," I responded.

"So, how are you?" he asked, which was something that he'd been asking every day since that happened.

"I'm not having bad dreams no more," I responded.

"That's good," he said. He never went into details of what happened to Kirk but, clearly, I knew that him and Raheem was behind his death.

"The autopsy report came back. It was said that Kirk drowned. Nova says that his family knows there had to be foul play, but I guess they aren't going to push the issue. I don't know why, but it's gotta be something deep within that family unit."

"That house had cameras all over it. So, I'm sure it was a lot of stuff they saw in the little time that Kirk had been living in that house. However, my cousin is a wiz kid when it comes to shit like that. He cut out over a week of footage. So, I'm sure they saw everything up until the cameras went out. The only thing is that they saw a lot more than they're telling and that's why they don't want to look any deeper into his case. It'll be some grimy shit that'll come out about their son. I'm sure. I can tell they're not the kind of people that want others looking at them sideways."

"You got a point," I said.

"So, y'all had the footage deleted? Y'all don't bullshit," I said with a shake of the head. I needed to make sure that we always stayed on their good side. Niggas like them were rare and couldn't be fucked with. They had so much at stake and probably had been doing shit like this since the beginning of time. I was sure it didn't just start with Heavy and Rah's generation. That kind of shit had been in play for a long time.

"We just don't play about the people we love. You cross us, you're fucked. But, if you're a genuine friend, then you're a friend for life. Nobody can fuck that up but you."

"I heard that." I smiled, now using his own saying on him. At that moment, a knock was heard at the door.

"Must be your girls," Heavy said. "I'll get on outta here."

"Okaaaay," I said, as he leaned over and kissed me on the lips. Something about this nigga made my pussy wet, but we still hadn't fucked yet. I didn't want to rush it. I figured in due time. I walked him to the door. He stopped and hugged me, smelling all good and shit, before walking out.

"Wassup Heavy?" Yaz said.

"Hey Heavy," Nova spoke with a smile.

"Wassup ladies?" Heavy spoke back with a friendly smile. "A'ight babe, I'll call you later. Y'all hold it down and have fun," he added.

We walked back in the house, as Nova handed over some paperwork with a big ass smile on her face. "What's this?" I asked.

"Just read it," she responded.

"Girl, I'm so happy for you," Yaz said, giving her a hug.

It didn't take me long to see that it was the deed to the condo as I screamed out in joy. "YAAASSSS BIH, YASSSSS!!" I let out.

"I know, right; now, you don't have to move," she said with a big smile on her. "However, you will have a roommate because I'm coming back to move in the second bedroom. Ya know, since this shit is mine," she teased.

"Girl, you can get whatever bedroom you want, as long as I ain't gotta move," I responded, as Nova plopped down on the red leather sectional. Yaz sat down beside her and grabbed the remote to the TV.

"Keep the bedroom you're in. I don't wanna be in the same bedroom that Kirk and I shared anyway. Plus, both bedrooms are master suites, so it's a win win either way."

This news had certainly made my day, as I smiled inside and out. However, my mouth partly dropped open, as the reality hit of what I was holding in my hand. "Wow, I can't believe he left you this."

"Me either," Nova responded back. "It's so crazy though but, the night I went over, he said he had some paperwork to handle before he left town. I think he was talking about this. I'm most certain he was going to change the deed, probably back to his own name."

"I believe you're right," Yaz chimed in. "But, it was too late. He didn't live long enough to do it."

"I know. That's the sad part about it, but at least you got something out of his ass," I said with a nod of the head. "I really hate that happened to him, but Kirk was a real jerk to a lot of people. Had he not been the one floating in that lake, it would've been you."

"I know and that's the only thing that makes me feel better about this whole thing," Yaz agreed.

"Me too," Nova sadly said. "I can't believe he would've actually killed me. However, his actions from that night told me that he had something planned and it wasn't good. I know that."

"Well, his plans backfired thanks to Rah and Heavy," I said.

"Has Rah said anything about that night, anything that would've pertained to them being the ones that saved you?" Yaz asked.

"Honestly, he only says enough. He doesn't go into details or anything like that."

"So, it's clear that he really likes you. I mean, he came to your rescue."

"I guess, but Rah is not your average guy. He straight up said that he's not the dating type, so y'all know how that is."

"Do I?!!" I chimed in with a shake of the head. " Heavy is a handful himself. He's the same way. Let me tell y'all about his lil bitch."

"Oh, Lord, feels like I'm gonna need a glass of wine."

"Well, we have the good shit today, thanks to him. He bought us Olive Garden to eat and three bottles of their house wine."

"Bitch, why you ain't been said something? I'm hungry as hell," Nova said, now heading into the kitchen with Yaz following her.

"I knew I smelled good food the minute I walked in. I thought yo' ass was whipping up something for us," Yaz said.

"Not today Bitches. I got a lot on my mind. Well, at least I don't have to worry about moving now," I said. I began to fix me a plate along with them. "Nova, are you sure you don't mind me being your roommate?"

"Girl, not at all. I couldn't ask for a better roomy, unless it was Yaz."

"Aww Cousin, I'm gonna miss you though. Don't y'all hate if I be over here more than my own crib now,"

Yaz laughed.

"You know we're like the three amigos, so it won't matter at all." Nova grinned.

Once we fixed our plates, we ended back up in the entertainment room, sitting down to eat. "So, let me tell y'all about last night."

"Yes girl, we're all ears," Yaz said, sipping from her glass of wine.

"I know I am," Nova concurred.

"Well, so, last night, I was at Heavy's nice ass house and he had to keep his daughter. She is so beautiful by the way," I said with a smile just thinking about the little one.

"Aww, so he didn't mind bringing her around you. How old is she?"

"I believe she's three," I answered. "Anyway, we were having a lovely time. We watched Despicable Me 1, 2, and 3." I grinned. "That seems to be her favorite cartoon I do believe."

Yaz and Nova laughed.

"I can't believe that Tam was playing mommy dearest," Nova chimed in while chewing her food.

"Girl, it was only for the day, but I did enjoy being around her and her father. It allowed me to see his daddy skills in action and I must say that he's good with it."

"Well, that's good. At least you'll know how things will be if you ever get pregnant by him," Yaz said.

"Which is something that I'm definitely not thinking about right now."

"I feel you, me either Tam," Nova said.

"So, back to my story. Her mom comes to pick her up last night and, when she saw me there, she had a fucking fit."

"She didn't know you were there?"

"From what I gathered, Heavy told her that I was there, but I believe it pissed her off to know that I was still there when she arrived. Nevertheless, she started cussing him out, like he had fully disrespected her in the worst way. She was yelling at the top of her lungs, had the poor baby crying and shit. It was crazy."

"So, what happened? What did Heavy do?" Nova pondered.

"He kept telling her to chill out, but she wasn't trying to hear it. She told him that he'd never see their daughter again if he was going to be bringing her around another bitch."

"BITCH?! I know damn well she ain't call you that?" Yaz chimed in.

"Oh yea, and she did more than that."

"So, Heavy kept telling her to chill out, but she wasn't having it. The bitch asked me did my lips taste like her pussy because he'd just had his mouth on it."

Yaz and Nova's eyes stretched open. "You have gotta be kidding me."

"Nawl, I'm so serious."

"What did you say?" they pondered at the same

time.

"Nothing," I said. "I wanted to rip the bitch head off but, when she said that, Heavy grabbed her by the arm and nearly drug her ass out the house. I don't know what he said once they were outside, but he came back in and apologized for her behavior. However, it wasn't long after that, I decided I should leave. I was pretty upset about the whole encounter, which brings me back to him buying this food for us. He's still trying to make up for that incident."

"Well, I ain't mad at him because this shit is good," Yaz said.

"I've had a taste for some Olive Garden, so homey came through then," Nova added.

"So, what if you have a run in with that lady again; then what you gonna do? I know your ass and you ain't gon' just let somebody keep trying you like that," Yaz said.

"You better believe it. If that shit ever happens again, Heavy is going to see a side that'll either turn him off or turn his ass on. Either way, I'm not holding back. The only reason she got away with that is because of her daughter being there. Let me catch that bitch by herself and I'm not gon' be so chill. I guarantee you that."

"I already know it," Nova said.

"Reminds me of this Beans chick that's pregnant by Smoke. This bitch just won't fucking quit. It's bad enough that she walked in on us fucking, but I believe she does stuff just to be relevant now. Like, for instance, Kirk's memorial service tomorrow. I was going to ride with y'all anyway, but I did wanna be there for my man too. However, he tells me that his mom wanted to ride with him. You know, to be there for her son, plus she treated Kirk like her own as well. But, how about this?" she said like the news was about to get juicier. "She also mentioned that Beans would be riding too."

"What? How did they come up with that?"

"Apparently, the mom and Beans are close. Once Beans shared the news about her being pregnant, then the mom has all kinds of things to say, like maybe Smoke and Beans need to be close because of the baby."

"Close as in them being together?"

"That's the only thing I can think of. I believe she's said more to Smoke than that, but he's only going to share what he wants me to know."

"Typical," I uttered.

"Anyway, he wanted to make sure that I was okay with Beans being there with him and his mom. Of course, I said I didn't mind, but y'all know I do. The shit is starting to piss me off, but I can't just let this woman walk in and take over. I mean, I love him. I don't care how long they've been friends."

"I feel you," Nova said. "And you shouldn't let her win. Fight for your man. Hell, it couldn't have been that serious if she had to hide the pregnancy for seven or eight fucking months anyway."

"Now, that I can agree with," I chimed in with a nod of the head. "These fucking relationships are a trip. I don't know what to say about them."

"And the funny thing is that we're all going through

some shit at the same damn time," Yaz said.

"What I tell you? We're like the three fucking amigos."

We laughed, just as Nova's phone alerted her of a text message. She read it with a smile.

"You good Sis?" I pondered.

"It's Raheem and he wants to know when I'll be coming to his house."

"Ohhhh, somebody's getting serious," I teased.

"Pump your brakes. I keep telling y'all that's it's not that simple or sweet. I guess I'll just have to go with the flow until I really know where we're headed in this relationship."

"It's nothing wrong with that Cuz. I can't blame you."

"So, when are you going to his house?" I asked.

"When I leave here," she answered. "You know it's something I was thinking about it and it's been on my mind since Kirk's death."

"What's that?" we asked at the same time.

"Kirk had a duffle bag full of money on his kitchen counter, but that money was gone the next morning when we were in the kitchen. I wanted to ask Raheem about it but decided not to. I mean, I didn't want to seem ungrateful, but I'm so curious to know what happened to it."

"Shit, you already know what happened to it. They fucking got it. Simple as that," I said.

"How much money was it?"

"It was a duffle bag full of money. Oh, how I wished I had gotten my hands on that. We really wouldn't have to worry about shit," Nova said.

"Just know if the money was taken, it was for good reason," Yaz said. "No damn telling, Kirk probably owed them that money."

"You got a point," Nova said. "I just need to be making my own money. I know working at the restaurant is cool, but I want more. I need to pay off these loans, so I can at least get my ass back in school. Plus, I have a lifestyle and y'all know it's not cheap."

"We knoooow," I clowned but was definitely serious.

"Something will work out for you. Even your dad knows that the restaurant isn't for you."

"But, he's the best daddy in the world and he's always looking out for me. I couldn't ask for better parents to be honest. I know they're gonna be so excited to know that I own a condo now. Like, who would've ever known that Kirk was even remotely thinking like that?"

"I know I wouldn't have known," I said. "That nigga is selfish as hell, so to do that... I don't know. He must've had his reasons."

"Well, it doesn't matter now. It's yours and that's all that counts."

"You're right Yaz." Nova said. "I can't even fully enjoy the moment because I still have to prepare myself for this memorial on tomorrow. Just because we'd gone our separate ways don't mean that I didn't have love for this man. I still cared deeply for him and just wanted him to get his shit together. We did have some fun times. It's just that his temper became too much for me over time and I couldn't just sit around and let a man think it was cool to put his hands on me."

"Shit, I feel you. The muthafucka would've been dead fucking with me," Yaz said with a slick roll of the eyes.

"We knoooow," I laughed. "Does Smoke know he has a lil gangster on his hands?"

"Oh trust, he knows. That's why his ass tread lightly. I will speak my mind if need be and I will whoop some ass if necessary. I hope that Beans don't ever pull a stunt like Heavy's baby mama or she'll regret it right there in that moment."

We laughed because we knew Yaz was a fool with it. She didn't look like the type, but she didn't mind fucking a bitch up.

"Anyway," Nova said, glancing down at her watch. "I need to be making my way out in this country, so I can see Raheem. A part of me is so glad that he wants us to talk, but I just have to maintain my feelings. I mean, I don't wanna be crushing too hard over his sexy ass and he is not feel the same way about me."

"I totally understand," I said. "Which is why I'm a little standoffish myself when it comes to Heavy. So, don't feel bad."

"Well, I won't be back over here tonight but, after this service tomorrow, I'll get moved in. I know I have to get a bedroom set first, but I'm sure I can get that. Hell, my credit is good." Nova smiled.

"Just let me know or don't," I teased. "Either way, I'm just happy as hell I ain't gotta move."

Yaz laughed. "Well, have fun Cuz. You deserve it. I'll see you when you get back."

"Okay," Nova said, giving us a hug; then, she left the house.

"Do you think they'll end up together?" I pondered while looking over at Yaz.

"Hell, I wish I could call it, but you just never know until you know."

I nodded my head. She was absolutely right. Life was unpredictable, especially when it came to love. I just wished us nothing but happiness, no matter what or who would come with it.

7

Raheem "Rah" Delgado

"I was thinking of going to Kirk's memorial tomorrow," Jose said, as I shot the nigga the side eye.

"For what, with his grimy ass? You don't owe that nigga no respect. None of us do," I stated.

"I just wanna go to make sure he's dead."

Heavy and I frowned. "What nigga?" I asked. "We know for a fact he's dead."

"I know, but I could've sworn I saw that nigga when me and Heavy was in the store yesterday."

"You talking about the gas station where I met Tam at to fill up her tank?"

"Yea," he responded.

"I know damn well you ain't losing your mind now after all the niggas we done took out the game." Heavy grinned with a shake of the head. "Nigga seeing ghosts and shit."

I grinned because the shit was kind of funny, but the expression on Jose's face was serious as hell.

"I'm just saying," Jose responded. "It looked like he followed Tam when she pulled out of the parking lot."

"Man, that could've been anybody," Heavy said.

I nodded my head. "Yea, it definitely could've been anybody. What was he driving?"

"A black on black Maybach," he answered.

"Well, we know that wasn't Kirk. A Charger and a Maybach aren't even in the same league."

"Yea, well, it was somebody that looked like him."

"Cuz, chill out. Kirk is dead, they're burying him tomorrow. You ain't gotta worry about that," Heavy said.

"I know, I know," Jose said. "This shit is crazy. My mind is definitely playing tricks on me."

"This nigga sees dead people," Heavy laughed out loud. "Let me call auntie and tell her to send your ass to seek therapy. We don't need you involved if this shit ever happens again."

"Man, don't fucking do me like that. You know I can handle this shit. This ain't new to me, my nigga. I was just saying."

"Yea, yea, I hear ya," Heavy responded while still grinning.

I just sat quietly listening to the two bicker back and forth with each other. Took me back to a time when we were kids growing up on a plantation full of Drug Lords. The men in the family taught us the rules of the game which consisted of respect, loyalty and honor. On the other hand, the matriarchs of the family showed us admiration, love and what it was to have a heart. In all, they groomed us to be well respected men that loved each other hard and always knew that family came first no matter what.

As yougans, we were always joking around but trying to prove that we had skills that the other didn't have. Talking shit was our specialty, but it was only to each other. Niggas outside the circle wasn't allowed that privilege. If they fucked with one, they fucked with all of us and nobody in their right mind wanted to do that. We grew up wealthy in money and rich in love when it came to our family. We were the heirs to our dynasty, and we were treated as such. My grandfather, a Mexican that carried on the legacy from his father, passed it down to my father who was the head of his generation and also known as the smoothest drug cartel that ever did it. He passed the torch on to me, even though he's still a major part of the business in all aspects. To this day, I aspired to be just like him. His brothers and cousins were his protectors and they would do anything for him. It was the same as my grandfather and his closest of kin. Now, it was the same for me. The organization was so tight knit and ran so smooth, which was why it was able to run as long as it had.

My brother initially held the reign being that he was older than me, but an unknown sickness started to attack his immune system, which caused him to step down to tend to his health. I didn't know how true it was because no one liked to speak about it. However, he was once in love with a woman that was said to be linked to the Russian Mafia, the same Mafia that had ties in my uncle's death. This said woman poisoned him, as a slow means of death that was plotted against my family. The only reason why I believed it was because it came from an exceptionally reliable source, my mom. It was her way of making sure that I was on top of any and everything, including the family secrets.

"So, how's Smoke doing? Have you talked to him?" Heavy asked.

"He's okay. I guess it took some time to take it all in, but we spoke earlier this morning on the phone and he's fine. I invited him to come out later and shoot pool with us, but he declined. He's mentally preparing for the services tomorrow and I completely understand. Just from his ways and habits, I can tell that he's a part of our bloodline. We love hard when it comes to us, and it was no different than his love for Kirk. He just knew that Kirk was a loose cannon and would explode in the worst way; it was just a matter of time. So, technically, he protected us not knowing why, while going against a nigga that was supposed to be his best friend."

"When I went to Kirk's territory to pick up his drop, the niggas started telling me how he was hating on Smoke taking over Underwood. Shit was unreal. I mean, damn, why speak ill about your boy to them niggas? They only respected him because of Smoke."

"I know," I agreed. "That's why I don't feel bad about what I did to him. The nigga wasn't loyal and needed to go. Simple as that," I said. "Y'all know I'm going to tell Smoke about that shit too."

"And you should," Heavy said. "That'll take some weight off his shoulders. That nigga was full of shit."

Jose simply shook his head. "I still need to make sure the nigga dead."

Heavy and I busted out laughing.

"Here this nigga goes again," Heavy clowned. "But, let me tell y'all about Simone's crazy ass last night. I was keeping my daughter, mind you for her. Not that I have any problems keeping my children—"

"Right," I uttered.

"So, I tells her that I had company."

"Company being Tam, right?"

"Right, and she acted like she was cool with it until she made it out here and seen Tam at my house. My niggas, this woman acted a straight fool in front of our daughter. She was pissed off to see me with another woman."

"Yea, but she knows y'all were never a couple," Jose chimed in a with curious expression.

"Exactly, so I don't know what the fuck the problem was. Okay, I can believe it was seeing me with another woman and probably having her around our child. But, I told her ass that before she got here. Hell, she acted cool about it. If I had known she was going to act like that, I would've met the bitch at the front gate on a golf cart and dropped my baby off to her ass."

I grinned to myself. Women could be unpredictable at times. "How did Tam react?"

"I must admit, Tam was rather G about it. It actually turned me on because she could've matched Simone's energy. However, she respected the fact that my daughter was there and turned the other cheek."

"Damn, you better be glad because shit could've gone way left."

"Hell, I thought it was, especially when Simone told her that if she kissed my lips, she was also tasting her pussy."

"She said that?" Jose chuckled.

"Hell yea, which meant that I had to admit that I'd just fucked her ass a couple of nights ago."

"Damn," I laughed. "That's some crazy shit. You know how women are. That's going to keep playing on her mental."

"Tell me about it," Heavy concurred. "I literally had to toss her ass out. I really wanted to rough her up, but she was lucky that my daughter was there."

"Saved by the bell," Jose joked.

"All I know is if it ever happens again, I won't be so nice."

"Try to keep your cool when it comes to women. They can be unpredictable. I mean, look at Keisha's ass." I grinned.

"You got jokes?" Jose asked, cutting me the side-eye but then laughing it off.

I glanced down just as my phone rang. I looked at the display screen to see that it was the guards at the gate calling. I smiled inside while answering it. "Wassup?"

"Ms. Nova Thang is here."

"Let her in," I said.

"That must be Nova," Jose teased. "I ain't seen a smile on your face like that since Ginger."

"Don't bring up Ginger. He gets in his feelings just

hearing her name," Heavy teased.

"Nigga please. I been moved on from that," I said with a slight chuckle. Nothing they could say would get to me now. My mind was too distracted thinking about Nova walking through the door.

"Aye, you still gonna offer her that position?"

"Hell yea," I answered. "That's the only way I'll know what she's really about."

"You don't think that's putting her in danger?"

"Not if she can handle it," I responded. "Plus, from what I saw when she shot at Kirk, I'd say she can handle it. Only she can tell me otherwise and, if that's the case, I'll be fine either way."

"I don't know. She just seems so sweet and not about that life," Jose chimed in.

"She is sweet, I know that. However, I got a feeling that she is about that life. She's just never had to sign up for anything like this."

"So, what makes you think she will?" Heavy asked.

"The money, the power, and to gain my trust—"

"And attention," Jose added.

"Hell, she already got that," Heavy teased.

"You're right, but he might even marry her after this. Who knows?" he clowned with a hearty chuckle while looking over at me.

"Yea, yea, you lame for that. I don't believe I'll ever get married. She gotta be someone seriously special for all that," I said with a laugh and a shake of the head. The doorbell rang, as I looked over at the fellas. "You ain't gotta go home, but you gotta get the fuck outta here."

They laughed. "I had a feeling that was coming next," Jose chimed in.

"A'ight, we'll catch up later," Heavy said as he and Jose headed out. "Send Nova in here when y'all go out."

"A'ight."

As I stood by the pool table awaiting her entrance, I sipped from my glass of Remy. I had thoughts of how I'd approach her with this proposition, but it was only one way and that was just to ask. Either she was down or not.

I sat my glass down on the edge of the pool table and picked up the pool stick, hitting the eight ball in the hole. I looked up from the table and saw Nova entering the room. She was beautiful. I loved her chic, laid-back style. Just sexy as hell. She sashayed straight over to me in a short mini skirt and a tight fitted tank top. She picked up a pool stick and smiled.

"I heard you giving out lessons this evening," she teased in a sweet tone. "I wanna learn everything you're teaching."

I grinned, trying not to blush. I had to maintain my gangster persona. "Wassup Mamacita? You come in here like you 'bout that life."

"What makes you think I'm not?" she asked as she attempted to hit one of the balls in the hole. It was a big miss and, instantly, she burst out laughing. It was so cute, she made me laugh. "See, that's why I need lessons."

"You're funny," I responded. "But, I got you." I

walked over and took the pool stick from her. "Another day for this, raincheck?"

"Definitely," she responded, as I wrapped my arms around her.

"Wassup Ms. Thang?"

"Nothing much, Mr. Delgado."

Her smile was contagious. Shawty had all my attention. I backed away from her, trying not to stare too deeply in her eyes. "You want something to drink?"

"I'll have what you got."

"I'm on Remy. You sure you want some of this?"

"Yep," she said, popping her lips like she could hang.

"Okay, yep," I mocked while walking over to the bar and fixing her a drink. "Chaser?"

"Just ice."

"Oh, so that's how you're feeling?"

"Definitely," she responded with a smile.

"Okay," I said back. "How was your day?"

"My day was fine, I guess. Let me tell you about my visit with Kirk's parents."

"Do tell," I said. "Come, sit down." I sat down on the white leather sectional that was facing the large 80-inch TV on the wall, as she walked over and sat down beside me. I propped my feet up on the white square ottoman in front of the sectional. We both had our drinks in our hands, as she sipped from hers and then scowled. "It's strong, ain't it?" I grinned.

"Hell yea," she chuckled. "Anyway, Mrs. Koban wants me to come to the services tomorrow."

"Well, were you planning on going anyway?"

"Yea, I was going. I'd thought about it since his death and decided that it was only right that I show up, since we were together for a few years. I guess I owe myself that closure as well."

"I understand."

"Anyway, she tells me that she put me in his obituary as a dear friend. I really didn't know how to take that being that he and I were over and our break-up was far from pleasant. However, I didn't say anything. If that makes her feel better, then fine. Plus, he left me the condo."

I frowned while sipping from my drink. "He left you the condo that y'all had moved out of?"

"Yes, I don't believe he intended on keeping it that way, but he died before he could change that. So, I have the deed to the condo. His mom gave it to me, to my surprise. I wasn't expecting that, but I'm grateful for it. God works in mysterious ways and now I have a home of my own that's paid for."

"He was good for something, I see. Congratulations. That's a nice ass condo."

"Thank you," she responded with a smile. "Over time I wanted to leave the place and move on to something else. I think because I felt like if we were in another space, Kirk would change. Silly me-"

"Was it bad memories in the condo?"

"Not all bad, but Kirk put his hands on me more than a few times. Some things I just didn't even talk about, but that's what made me want to leave. It's such a different space now. I believe Tam's touch and good energy definitely changed the atmosphere. Now, I can move in and keep that energy going."

"So, is Tam going to continue staying there?"

"Yea, she can be my roommate. I would never put her out just because the place is mine. She's like a sister to me. I'm going to move in the other bedroom, which is fine with me because she's in the bedroom that Kirk and I had. The second bedroom is a master suite also. They're the same square footage, both big and nice. I just used the second room for closet space and to lounge in when I wanted to get away from Kirk. I guess that's why I wanted a bigger house. It would be more rooms for me to hide in," she joked.

"I guess," I said with a shake of the head. "I'm just glad you're out of that situation now."

"You and me both," she agreed with a smile. "So, how have things been going for you?"

"Things have been pretty smooth, considering we lost one of our main runners. However, the loss was ultimately his loss, not entirely ours," I told her.

"I get it," she comprehended. "What are your plans for replacing him?"

I turned up my drink and looked in her eyes. This was the perfect moment for me to feel her out and see where she stood when it came to me and her. "Well, I have a proposition for you," I started in just wanting to make sure I worded this right. "If you're at all interested, I would like for you to take over Kirk's territory."

Nova's eyes widened. "YOU WHAT?"

"I would like for you to take over Kirk's territory. I know you could use the extra money and it's damn good money to be made. Plus, it gives us the opportunity to work together and for you to get in on a lucrative part of my family's business. Not only that, you'll have Smoke, Heavy, Jose and, more importantly, me watching your front and back to make sure that you're always safe. You can bring your girls in on it to help you, but all you'll really be doing is showing face and picking up drops. Sometimes, you'll check on the inventory and, of course, you'll have to meet the guys that'll be working for you. That way, they'll know you and will also have your back. So, what'll you say?" I asked.

I watched her body language; it seemed like she'd gotten a bit anxious with not expecting what I had just proposed. I didn't know if she'd say yes or no, but her answer would likely define where we stood from here on out. I just needed to know if she would ride for me because it was evidently clear that I would ride or die for her.

8

Nova Thang

I sat pondering over the proposition that Raheem had just given me. I sipped on my drink a few times until it was actually gone, while thinking about my next choice of words. It must've been a good ass reason for him to ask me this, something I never expected. I was shocked, to say the least.

"Well, um."

"You don't have to give me an answer today. Matter of fact, take as much time as you need."

"You sure you want me to do something like this? I mean, I know absolutely nothing about that," I said, referring to the drug game. "I only dated a man that was in the league."

"I understand."

"So, I wouldn't even know where or when to begin."

"I know, which is why I will guide, show you the ropes, introduce you to your team, and then let you run the territory on your own."

"Like a boss?" I teased but was serious at the same time.

He grinned with a nod of the head. "Yea, like a Boss."

"So, all I'll be doing is picking up the drops? I assume that's the money, right?"

"Right and, at least once a week, you need to make sure that the inventory is on point."

"Inventory?" I pondered.

"Yes, your territory has anywhere from fifteen to thirty blocks they move a week. Some territories are half that, some more; it just depends on the location. We run a large operation, very large, so we're particular about the people that run in our circle," he told me.

"So, how much are the drops?" I asked.

"The drops range from about fifty thousand to two-hundred thousand or more. It just depends."

My eyes stretched opened, as I looked at Raheem. "Fifty to two-hundred thousand?! That's a lot of money!"

"It is, but don't worry."

"How am I supposed to leave an area carrying that much money without anything happening to me?"

"Trust me, nothing will happen to you. There is always someone on standby watching you until you get back to your destination. We'll discuss that part when the time comes. This business has been running smoothly for decades. We've had a lot of fallen soldiers, a lot of retired soldiers, and some still in the game, simply because they love it and don't know no other life but this one. One thing you need to keep in mind is that things aren't quite what you may be imagining. This is nothing like TV or the movies. So, shake those thoughts out your head. We have frontline runners that know what they sign up for. They distribute the work and watch the block. The boys on the block make the runs and report back to the frontline runners. Only the top runners pick up the drops and check in with the frontline runners to make sure that everything is on point regarding their territory, including the supply. When your territory needs supply, Jose or Smoke will handle that. You will never touch the supply, only the bag."

"And the bag is the money?"

"The bag is the money or in other terms, the drop."

"So, technically, I would be a top runner? Top runners are the bosses in the game or of their territory, right?"

Raheem nodded his head. "Yea, you can say that because there is no one above them but me. Heavy, Jose and now Smoke are my partners," he answered but elaborated a little more. "I wouldn't be above you, though. I'd be in front, behind, and beside you."

Something about the way he put that made me smile inside, as it also appeared outside. As I sat contemplating what I would do or say about this newly proposed position, Raheem stood up and walked over to the bar. Instantly, my mind was blurred with visions of his fine ass. The nigga was mind blowing, tattoos everywhere, tall fit body like he worked hard on a farm or played basketball on a regular. He was handsome as hell and dressed like he had money. Although, now, he was wearing a plain white tee with black Balenciaga gym shorts and a pair of white Nike socks. Something so simple looked so damn good on him. His diamond cut chain matched his diamond cut Rolex, and all I could do was smile as he made his way back over to me. Holding the bottle of Remy, he poured a little more of the stiff drink in my empty glass.

"You good?"

"Yea," I responded. "Thank you."

"No problem," he said while pouring himself more of the Remy as well. He sat back down beside me. "I want you to know that I'm offering you this position because I trust you and, honestly, I want to work with you. I know I'm a very busy man, but I don't want you to think that this is the only way we'll be able to hang out or see each other. I really just want you on my team, any which way I can get you. So, if you don't take this offer, it won't sway my decision one way or the other when it comes to us. It's just so hard to trust people nowadays. I always knew to watch Kirk for some reason. He just never seemed to be the trusting type, and for good reason. He lied more than a few times and played with my money repeatedly. From this point on, I'm only surrounding myself with those I can wholeheartedly trust."

"I feel you. Kirk betrayed us all in his own way. Kind of sad if you ask me because he wasn't all bad. However, the bad seemed to outweigh the good in the end. I hate it came down to him losing his life, but I feel like it was either my life or his. Fortunately for my family and friends, it wasn't me."

"I don't know if I would've been able to handle that, so I'd rather not talk about it," Raheem said as he sipped on his drink.

I wanted to say something in response to that but

didn't exactly know what to say. All I knew was that somewhere along the way, I'd made a good impression on Raheem. One that I would even say tugged at his heart. I didn't want to overstep my boundaries in thinking in that manner because he was the kind of man that masked his feelings well. The only thing I could do was go by his actions because those were quite telling.

I stood up from my relaxed position on the sectional and headed over to the pool table. Once again, I pick up the pool stick. "Rack 'em up."

Raheem glanced back at me with a smile. "So, really wanna do this, huh?"

"Yep," I answered, as he got up and made his way to the pool table. "Rule number one, for every hole we miss, we have to answer a question. It can be any question and we have to truthfully answer it."

"Any question?"

"Yes, any question and, if I win, I get whatever I want tonight."

Raheem's curiosity was peeked, as he raised a questionable eyebrow. "Whatever you want?"

"Yes, whatever my little heart desires."

"Okay, and if I win?" he asked.

"If you win, I'll take you up on your proposal, no more questions asked. You just lead the way."

"Oh yea?"

"Yea," I responded with a smile.

"Sounds interesting," he said, pulling all fifteen billiard balls out of the pocket holes and racking them in the triangle holder.

"Let's make this game even more intriguing," I chimed in.

"Do tell."

I smiled from ear to ear. "Every time we miss a hole, we have to take a shot of Remy."

Raheem shot me a handsome smile. "Oh, this game is fun already."

"Oh, and that's not all."

"Give it to me," he said.

"Every time we miss a hole, we have to take off a piece of clothing," I added.

"Ohhh, you gotta be kidding me. Does a sock count as a piece of clothing?" He laughed out loud.

"Yes, one sock is considered a piece of clothing.

"You know I can already picture you naked."

"So, you got jokes huh?" I laughed.

"Lots of 'em," he chuckled, now holding his pool stick in his hand like he was ready for war. "Any more rules that I need to be aware of?"

"Nope," I answered. "Not yet anyway."

"So, ladies first."

"Okaaaay," I said, holding my pool stick like a pro. "I gotta break the balls, right?"

"Yea and, for your sake, you better hit a pocket."

I giggled. "Okay, so if the eight ball lands in a pocket before all the balls are cleared, that means that you automatically lose."

He grinned. "Another rule, huh?"

"Yea, but that's also a real rule, right?"

"Oh, so you do know a lil something about pool. You're not trying to fool me, are you?"

"Not at all," I answered with a shake of the head. I really didn't know shit about pool. I just wanted this to be a fun game of getting to know each other. "Okay, here goes nothing," I said while bending over the pool table and giving it my best shot. I stood back watching as if I'd really done something when I barely moved any balls. The shit was quite funny to me, as I bust out laughing.

"Somebody needs work," Raheem chuckled. "Now, it's time to follow the rules."

I jokingly rolled my eyes, picking up my glass and guzzling the Remy down.

"Damn, that was a lil more than a shot," he said with surprised eyes, as I scowled like it was the worst taste in the world.

"That shit is strong as hell," I said, now softening my look. "Okay, what's your question?"

"What's your mom's full name?" he asked me.

"Oh, you're taking it easy, I see. My mom's full name is Noreen Pierre Thang."

"Pierre? That's her maiden name?"

"Yep," I answered as I took off one of my UGG slides.

"And she's coming out of her clothes," he teased. "Well, shoes first of course."

I grinned. "Your turn." Just as I expected, he hit one ball that hit another ball and two balls landed in a pocket hole. "Oh, you're good, good," I said.

"I'm a'ight," he teased. "So, what happens now? Do I go again like in a regular game of pool?"

"Yes, let's keep some of the rules the same." I smiled. Plus, I just wanted him to miss a damn pocket hole.

"Okay, sounds good to me," he said and, back to back, he hit two more pockets. "Sheesh, we're down to eleven balls now."

"I know." Raheem grinned. Again, he pocketed another ball, leaving ten balls on the table. "You sure you wanna keep this going?"

"Yes, just miss already," I teased.

This time when he leaned down to hit a ball, I walked up behind him and slid my hand between his legs, and damn was I surprised at what I touched. He was certainly just as caught off guard because he missed a hole. I jumped up with excitement. "Whew Chile, you finally missed one."

Raheem laughed out loud. "You cheated."

"Not true, all is fair in love and war" I responded with laughter. "Drink up."

Raheem turned up his drink. "Okay, what's your question?"

"Hmmm, have you ever been in love?" I asked.

"You go straight for the juggler, I see."

I chuckled. "Well, what can I say."

"I've never been in love, but I've loved once," he answered.

"Mm-kay," I responded, just as Raheem pulled off his white tee.

"OMG," I whispered. His body was tatted all over. Full chest, stomach, arms and back, as he turned in a circular motion.

"Is this what you want?"

"Yep," I quickly responded while seductively staring his fine ass up and down.

"Now, your turn."

I wasted no time, scratching the damn table while missing another pocket hole. "Damn, I need lessons for real."

Raheem grinned. "You need more than lessons."

I laughed out loud. "Oh, you keep jokes on deck, I see."

"Never know when I might need one."

"Okay, well shoot. What's your question?"

"What age did you lose your virginity?"

"Oh, you're tryna come for me now, huh?" I teased. "But, it's cool. I was eighteen," I answered, as he poured me a shot to guzzle down. I pulled off my other shoe.

Raheem glanced down at my feet. "Cute," he said with a wink.

"Thanks," I responded. Back to back to back, Raheem landed three more holes, leaving seven balls on the table. I sat on the side of the pool table and crossed my legs. I needed to distract him any way possible. He looked over at me with a handsome smile.

"Nice legs," he teased. "And thighs," he added.

I blushed while watching him land another pocket hole. Shit was getting real and, just when I thought it was game over for me, Raheem missed one.

I laughed. "Thank goodness," I said, but I figured he did it on purpose. He was way too good not to play along. Without me even asking, he turned up his shot, and then removed a sock. I playfully rolled my eyes. "You could've given me a little more than that."

He laughed. "I'm just playing like you."

"Yea, yea," I teased. "So, when did you lose your virginity?"

"When I was thirteen."

"Thirteen?! DAMN! I bet you're experienced."

Raheem laughed. "Your turn."

"I knowww," I sang and grabbed the pool stick like I was about to show his ass what time it was. I looked over at him with a silly smirk. "You ready for this?"

"As ready as I'll ever be," he answered, and then I leaned down, eyed the ball I wanted to hit, and hit it. I hit it so hard that it went straight for a corner pocket and then stopped right at the edge of it. "What the fuck?!" I let out.

Raheem chuckled out loud while shaking his head.

"You tried ma."

"Damn," I uttered.

"What's your favorite color?" he asked me, as I picked up the bottle and gulped my shot. "Damn, you doing it like that?" He grinned.

"Yep, and yellow," I responded. By this time, I'd started to feel my liquor a lot, a lot. I only had on a tank top, a fitted mini skirt, and a pair of Fenty thongs with the matching yellow bra set."

"Take it off, take it off," Raheem jokingly chanted.

"You sure you want me to do this?"

"Damn right I'm sure," he answered. "You made the rules."

"Okaaaaay," I said while deciding to come out of my tank top.

Raheem looked over at me with a smile on his face. "I see why yellow is your favorite color. Nice," he complimented me and then leaned down with his pool stick as if watching me half naked was nothing he hadn't seen before. Before I knew it, he had cleared all the balls off the table except for three.

"So, you're gonna win this, I see."

"Yea, you're gonna lose Mamacita. Sorry 'bout that," he teased, but he missed a hole. Again, I figured he did it on purpose.

"Hmmmm," I said like I was thinking of what to ask him, as he wasted no time drinking from the bottle this time. He took off the other sock. "Do you really like me?"

"Yes," he responded. "Your turn."

"You think you're slick."

"Just a lil bit." He grinned.

Of course, I attempted, and I missed the damn hole again. I sucked at playing pool, and Raheem enjoyed every minute of me losing.

"Do you see yourself being with a nigga like me?" he questioned, as I turned up the bottle again.

"I sure do. I can see myself being your woman, your baby's mother, your other half, your ride or die," I carried on with my drunk ass.

Raheem grinned. Apparently, I was quite funny to him.

"So," I said while slipping out of my skirt. "I hope you like what you see." As my skirt fell to the floor, Raheem's eyes widened with interest.

"Very much," he responded.

"Your turn," I said, knowing that the three balls left on the table was the end of this little game that I'd started.

"So, if I win, you're going to run the territory for me, right?"

"Yep," I responded.

"And, if you win--"

"I get whatever my little heart desires," I cut in.

Raheem smiled and leaned over the pool table and took his best shot, straight at the eight ball. My eyes widened, thinking he had a trick up sleeve if he hit the

112

eight ball. Maybe it's going to hit the other three balls simultaneously, they'd hit their pockets, and then I'm out. But, to my surprise, the eight-ball landed straight in the pocket hole. I jumped up like a kid in a candy store, climbed my drunk ass up on the pool table and started doing the snake. Yes, I took it way back, seductively swaying my upper body from side to side, snapping my fingers and all while dancing like I'd really did something.

"So, I guess that's your victory dance?" He teased, standing there grinning with his arms crossed.

"I won, baby. I won," I sang, still dancing.

"So, since you won, what is it that your pretty lil heart desires? What do you really want Ms. Thang?" he pondered, watching me with a serious stare and waiting for an answer.

While standing almost naked in my yellow bra and panty set and watching the nigga I'd been dreaming about since I first laid eyes on him, I responded, "I want you."

9

Raheem "Rah" Delgado

This woman was standing on top of my twenty-thousand-dollar pool table and I ain't have shit to say about it. A nigga couldn't lean on my shit funny without me looking at him funny, yet Nova could take the whole damn table home and I wouldn't say a word. She was hella cute and adorable doing ole school dances and twirling in a circle, enjoying her win.

"Come here," I said, reaching for Nova's hand as she smiled at me. She walked to the edge of the table, pussy damn near staring me right in the face through her lace yellow thong. She smelled like an edible arrangement, had my dick about to jump out of my gym shorts.

I reached up to help her down, but found my hands palming her ass cheeks instead. She grabbed the top of my head like she was begging for it, as I buried my face in her most sacred hot spot. I picked her up with her legs wrapped around my head and continued sucking through her undies. The sexy sounds of her moans caused me to turn up even more. I ripped her thong off, tasting her sweet juices flowing inside my mouth, and then laid her back on the pool table. With her legs spread from east to west, I began to devour her goods like a lion enjoying the delectable meat of its prey. I had a big appetite and the dish Nova was serving I could snack on all night.

I traced my tongue around her clit in a circular gentle motion and slurped on it like a slushie. I could feel her heartbeat through the pulsation of her pussy lips, as the intense feeling caused an unexpected orgasm.

"Aaaaaaaah fuuuuck," she let out in the sexiest moan ever.

Nova's thighs gripped my head like she was trying to suffocate me, but she didn't know I'd die just to keep making her cum. As I maneuvered around her playground, my tongue found its way sliding down her rear end, as I toyed with her emotions, physically and mentally. I wanted to explore every inch of her body, causing her legs to tremble and shake like an earthquake. Shit was getting real as she called out my name, repeatedly. Remy and weed fueled the adrenaline that was pumping through my veins. I'd had lots of women in positions like this often, but none got the kind of attention that I was giving Nova. I wanted her to know that I was fully tuned in and ready for whatever.

As I finished feasting on every hole below her waist, Nova pulled me up, grabbing my face and slipping her tongue in my mouth. I could feel her body begging for more, but I wasn't sure if I wanted to give it to her. It wasn't because of me, but because of her. I didn't want her to get too locked in without knowing what all came with being with a man like me. I was a man that a lot of people feared. I was a gangster at heart and a thug in the streets. I would kill for the ones I loved and go to war against anybody that disrespected me. Even though I was rather cool-tempered and laid back, I could also get rowdy and hostile at the drop of a dime. I just needed Nova to know what she was signing up for because I wasn't trying to take this to another level for nothing. I stopped mid-action of Nova trying to take my shorts off.

"Hold up," I told her.

"Shhhhhh," she immediately said, putting her index finger up to my lips. "I don't need a long speech about am I sure or is this something I really want to get myself into. I don't wanna be reminded of what type of guy you are. I know and I'm not doing this because I'm expecting something in return or an exclusive relationship with the one and only bad boy Raheem Delgado. Please, I need this, and I'd rather get it from you than that damn battery-operated vibrator that Yaz gave me."

I grinned, while thinking this woman had me turned the fuck up. She was saying all the right things, so it was only right that I gave her what she was asking for. I slid my shorts and my boxer briefs off at the same time and held my python in my hand. I softly stroked it as the anticipation of fucking Nova had me excited and ready. As I slid inside the most precious place on her body, Nova's warm compressed temple gripped me tightly.

Ahhhhh, I let out in my mind. This shit was better than I ever could've imagined.

"Yes," Nova whispered. I could tell she needed this, and I was glad she was getting it from me and not some other unlucky nigga. Giving it to her slow and steady was exactly what the doctor ordered because she couldn't get enough. Throwing it back and moaning in my ear was only turning me on more and more. I began kissing her just to throw off the sensation of wanting to bust one but, the more Nova kissed back, the more aroused I got. Feeling her throwing it back on me and calling my name was doing something to my mental.

"Raheem."

Every time my name escaped her lips, I'd go deeper and deeper. I wanted to reach her soul, so she'd know that she was dealing with a real one. As I deep stroked her world, she aggressively switched positions and ended up on top. She was riding this wood like she missed it, but she ain't never had it til now. She began kissing on my chest while still giving me the ride of a lifetime. While straddling me, she turned backwards and started giving it to me from the back. I grabbed her butt cheeks, watching my pipe slide in and out of her. Cream covered my shaft, as her river flowed like a leaking faucet. Ms. Thang leaned forward, grabbing my legs right below kneecaps and began bouncing that ass up and down.

Ahhhhhh damn, I thought as my eyes rolled in the back of my head. She was turned up and I was turned the fuck on. Watching that ass twerking out of control had me feeling like we were in an X-rated video. I grabbed her by the waist, switching positions. She was now face down, ass up and I was packing her with everything I had. I couldn't stop; shit was too good. I was stuffing her slippery slope like a Thanksgiving turkey, and boy was I thankful for the gift she was giving me. I know we'd been going at it for more than an hour, moving from the pool table to the sectional sofa, and now to the bedroom. I was in between her legs, stroking her desires while entertaining her ego. I hadn't planned on going in like this, but I couldn't help myself. She had me cornered and didn't even know it. I was all in but, at this point, the ball was in her court.

After about another thirty minutes, she started squirming like she was trying to hold back, but I knew what that meant. She was about to blow and, hell, so was I. The minute she let on that she was cummin', I let it go too. We came at the same damn time, both breathing hard while trying to maintain our composures.

"Damn, that was the best dick I've ever had," Nova acknowledged. I grinned a little, kind of feeling myself but I could tell.

"I must admit, it was certainly good as hell."

"Glad you enjoyed yourself because if I had it my way, we'd be doing this three times a day."

"Woah, slow yo' roll shawty," I joked.

She laughed. "Stop playing. You know you wouldn't mind."

"You're right. I wouldn't mind, but that's only in a perfect world."

"Look, don't kill the vibe. Right now, the world is perfect and that's all that matters."

"I'll go along with that," I told her. Honestly, I didn't want the night to end, but that was just wishful thinking. I wanted to keep her as close to me as possible, but that was only if she played her cards right. She was given a damn good hand; I just didn't know what she'd do with it. She snuggled up in my arms, something I hadn't done with a woman in a long time. It felt foreign but good. She smelled so damn sweet, as I sniffed her hair and planted a soft kiss on the top of her head.

"So, since you won the game, by default," I added, as she grinned, "that means that my proposal is out the window. I'm just curious though. Do you plan on taking me up on my offer or not?" I asked, trying to feel her out. As I laid there waiting for her to respond, the next thing I heard was a light snore. I grinned to myself; she was just laughing and, now, she was sound asleep. I kissed her again with a smile on my face. The night couldn't have ended any better.

*****

I woke up the next morning, as I stretched my arms out. I was feeling pretty good. The night had gone way better than planned or expected. I looked over to the side of me to notice that Nova wasn't there. I sat up in the bed, thinking that she might've been in the bathroom freshening up. However, once out the bed and scoping out the scene, she wasn't there either. Instead of looking all over the place for her, I picked up my cell phone and called her. On the first ring, she answered.

"I was wondering when you'd wake up."

I could hear her beautiful smile through the phone. The shit was contagious, causing me to smile back.

"Good morning Beautiful."

"Hey, good morning Handsome," she responded.

"I woke up and saw that you weren't lying next to me? Have you left or are you still in this house somewhere?" Honestly, my house was big as hell. She could've been anywhere. So, the smart thing was to get her on the phone.

She chuckled. "Well, I not only kissed you before

leaving, I also left you a lil some, some too."

"Oh yea?" I pondered with a raised eyebrow. "Why didn't you just wake me? I could've walked you out."

"Because you were sleeping so peacefully, I didn't want to bother you."

"Next time, just bother me, okay."

"Yes sir," she teased. "Well, I only slipped out because I have to get ready for this memorial service." She sighed. "Not that I'm looking forward to it, but I guess that's the least I can do for his parents."

"Damn, I totally forgot about that. My head was in the clouds this morning. I just didn't even think about that."

"My head was in the clouds too, until Yaz called me to make see why I hadn't come home."

"Your phone rang and I didn't hear it?"

"Yep."

Damn, I always slept light as a feather. I knew my ass was slipping. I guess that's what it felt like to be in a peaceful state, surrounded by genuine company. "I must've drank too much."

"Yea, blame it on the alcohol, as if it couldn't have been this good good."

I laughed. "Oh, you got jokes I see."

"Just a few." She grinned.

"Well, uh, it could've been that wet wet," I teased back.

"Okaaay, could've been," she mocked with laughter.

"No but, seriously, I really enjoyed your company. It was like a breath of fresh air being with you. I've not had that much fun in a long time from the company of a woman."

"Oh really?" she asked in a playful tone.

"Yes, really," I responded with a smile. "So, not trying to change the subject, but are you okay? I mean, I know you have a long day ahead of you."

"Yes, I do, but the only thing that's on my mind is going to this memorial and getting back home. I'm not sticking around no longer than I must. I'm not going over to his parents' house afterwards either."

"If that's how you feel, then don't go. You're not obligated to go to his funeral, let alone spend any more time with his parents after the fact. You're doing this out of the kindness of your heart. It wasn't like you and the nigga were together."

"I know," she agreed. "That's the main thing that bothers me. Plus, knowing that he had some dark plans for me also plays on my mind. I'm well aware that if it wasn't him, it would've been me. His intentions were to drug me and then have his way with me. No damn telling what all that consisted of."

"I don't wanna think about it," I cut in. I couldn't fathom the thought of anything happening to her, especially not at the hands of his pussy ass. I wanted to tell her to fuck going to pay her respects, but I decided against it. I could be very cold when it came to shit like that, however, I couldn't tell her what she could or couldn't do. Maybe this was closure for her, at least those were the only thoughts that made me feel better about this shit.

"Well, afterwards, can I see you? It would be the only thing that would make me feel better when this is all over."

"We have weekly family dinners where the majority of everyone that lives on the estate link up and go over business, eat good, and discuss what's going on. They usually run pretty late," I told her, "BUT-"

"Oh, there's a but?"

"Yes, it is," I responded. "I'll make sure to leave early to be with you," I told her. This wasn't like some random request from a bitch that just wanted some dick or money. This was something that was important to her; therefore, it was important to me too.

"You just made me smile."

"Those are my intentions."

"Well, job well done," she told me, causing me to smile.

"About last night and that proposition you offered me-"

"Don't worry about that. I totally understand if that ain't something you want to involve yourself in. Plus, that's not conversation that we need to have right now. That can wait till later."

"So, things wouldn't change if I don't take the proposition?"

"No," I responded, but the main reason for me

offering her that position was so she could be a part of my business and in knowing what comes with that. I didn't want to really start liking her, then she left me while I was asleep like Ginger did. Therefore, if she knew what she was signing up for, I could see if she was really down for a nigga or not.

"You sure about that?"

"Yea," I answered. "I do think it's best if we take things slow though. I don't wanna get all in and then things go left."

"Why would they go left?"

"I don't know. Shit happens," I told her.

"Well, I don't mean to change the story, but I was up pretty early. Only because I was so anxious about this memorial service today. Then, Yaz called and I couldn't go back to sleep. So, I have a lil treat for you downstairs in the microwave."

I frowned. "In the microwave?"

"Yea," she answered.

"A'ight, what kind of treat? Did you cook for ya boy?"

"I did a lil some, some while you were sleeping like a baby."

"Nooooo, stop it," I said with a shake of the head. How the hell did I sleep through all of that?

"You don't keep much in your fridge, but I did my thing. All you have to do is warm it up."

"A'ight," I responded while heading down the

stairs. I figured it was time to let her go. I didn't want to consume her morning, knowing she had to get ready. "Well, get yourself together and call me when you get home and settled."

"I will."

"You can call me before then if need be," I assured her.

"Okay," she said, and we ended the call.

Once in the kitchen, I walked straight over to the microwave. I couldn't really smell any food, so I didn't know what lil something Nova had cooked for me. I opened the microwave to see a folded note sitting in front of the plate. After removing the note, I peeped the stack of pancakes topped with strawberries and whip cream. It wasn't until I saw the pancakes that I smelled its deliciousness. I smiled, thinking that shawty had pulled this one off without a hitch. I liked her style and how she had a way of pleasing me. I unfolded the note and couldn't help but smile even bigger after reading what it said.

I know I won the game last night, but you won my heart. Being that I won, I didn't have to take you up on your offer. However, I want to. I want to know what you do, how you make your living, what comes along with that territory. I believe if I can hang in something of that nature, then no telling how far that could take us as a couple. No, I'm not saying that we're a couple just yet, but I'm definitely speaking it into existence and manifesting all the great things that comes with this budding relationship. I look forward to you teaching me the ropes and in taking on this new journey. Hope you enjoy your pancakes, strawberries, and whip cream. After all, that's all you had in your kitchen to cook. Lol Genuinely Yours, Ms. Thang.

10

Rashad "Smoke" Rivers

"You okay son? I cooked your favorite because I knew today would be hard on you. I know it's not much, but that's the least I could do."

I looked over at my mom and then down at the plate of delicious food. She had definitely cooked my favorite: collard greens full of meat, dressing, macaroni and cheese, grilled chicken, and sweet candy yams. She always did her thing in the kitchen. I didn't understand why she never pursued a career in opening her own soul food restaurant.

"You did good today," I heard her say. I knew she was trying to make small talk, but I wasn't the least bit in the mood for any kind of conversation, didn't matter what it was about. I had just buried my best friend, my brother. It was one of the hardest things I had to witness. On top of that, I was struggling with the thought of my mom keeping such a huge secret from me. It's like my world changed overnight. Everything I thought I knew, I didn't. Everything I thought was right, was wrong. My head was all over the place, as I sat there staring off into space.

"Did you hear what your mama said?" Beans asked, as I snapped back to reality while looking over at her.

Hell, just seeing her and that big ass stomach was also another thing added on my plate. All of this shit seemed unreal but, somehow, I had to get it together. "Rashad?"

"I hear you," I finally said.

"Well, did you hear your mama talking to you?"

I shot her the side-eye. "What you think?" I asked.

Beans frowned with an expression that I was very familiar with. "Look, don't get an attitude with me. I know you're going through some things, but I won't be the person you lash out at."

"Alright y'all. Don't start that mess in here today. Reminds me of when y'all were teenagers with all that back and forth arguing. Never would I have thought that y'all's friendship would've flourished into my first grandbaby," Mama said.

"Me either," I uttered.

"You got that part right, especially with him moving on so fast with somebody else," Beans slid in.

Mama cleared her throat. It was as if she knew the shit was about to start up again, so she cut in. "As long as y'all can co-exist in the same space and put this baby first, y'all will be fine."

"We first gotta sit down and talk about this, being that I'm just finding out about it."

"Well, I agree son. Beans, why didn't you come forward when you found out?"

"I had my reasons," Beans responded with a bit of an attitude.

"Alrighty then," Mama said with a bit of sarcasm, as I simply shook my head. I didn't want things to be awkward between us. I wanted to be able to get along with my son's mother. Plus, Beans was like my best friend, I didn't see a reason as to why we couldn't make that happen.

"Aye, can you come by my spot tomorrow so we can finally talk about this situation? I think the sooner, the better."

"I couldn't agree more." Mama nodded.

"Yea, I can do that. Plus, I definitely think this is a conversation between me and you," Beans responded. It was almost like a sneak dig at my mama, but she could have that. I wasn't in the mood for her petty behavior. I knew her reasons behind it and that was also something I would need to address the minute we sit down to talk.

"Guess I'll leave then. We'll talk tomorrow," she said, giving me an uncaring hug and just nodding her head at my mama.

"A'ight, I'll text you later," I said, as she made her way to the front door. Normally, I would've walked her out, but not this time. I didn't like her funky ass attitude or how she'd been acting and that shit had to change if we were to co-exist as parents together.

"What's her problem?"

I glanced over at my mom while taking a bite of my food. "You already know," I answered.

"I know she can't be mad about Yaz sitting next to you at the funeral. What she expected? I mean, I know she's your baby mama, but Yaz is your girlfriend. Of course, any girlfriend would want to be there for their man at a time like that."

"Which is something I thought she would've understood. Guess I was wrong."

"Well, you need to talk to her about that, so she can go ahead and shake that evil spirit out her system. If you plan on being with Yaz, then she needs to accept that. I'm sure it has taken a lot for Yaz to accept the fact that she's pregnant by you, but that don't seem to bother her as much as I thought it would."

"It bothers her, but she handles it as well as can be expected."

"Well, she's doing a damn good job," Mama said. "Do you plan on having a blood test with the baby?"

I frowned. "Honestly, I didn't even think about it. However, she says it's mine, so I believe her."

"Which is all the more reason for you to have one."

At that moment, I put my fork down, swallowing the remnants of my food. Thinking about a blood test led my thoughts to being raised by a man that I thought was my father when, in actuality, it was a lie. I mean, why would Rah, Heavy and Jose bring that to my attention if it wasn't true? As I now sat consumed in those thoughts, mama called out.

"You alright son?" she pondered. "I know you have a lot on your mind, but I can tell it's something deeper than your issues with Beans."

"I'm glad you noticed," I said, just ready to get this shit off my chest. "Who is my real father?"

Mama frowned with uncertainty, as she stared at me. "What are you talking about?"

"I just want to know who my real father is."

"Why would you—"

"Mama, please, is Jerry my father?"

"Of course, he's your father."

"So, how come my last name ain't Harris, but he's my father and was once your husband?"

She nervously chuckled. "Boy, is that your concern, your last name? You know why but, if I gotta explain it again, I will. We weren't married when I had you, so you got my last name. We just never changed it."

I sat in silence, watching her open a cabinet and pull out a bottle of Whiskey. She grabbed a glass and poured herself a drink. Without hesitation, she turned it up. I simply shook my head, as I watched her pour up another drink. She turned to look at me with a serious expression.

"I don't know where you're going with this, but I'm hoping you're over it. You just watched your best friend being buried today. I think that dealing with Beans and the baby and having just gotten serious in a relationship with Yaz has you all over the place. You're trying to find something to take your mind off of the things that you don't want to think about. But, asking about your father when you already know who he is ain't it. He may not have been the best man in the world, but he's still your father. I understand that y'all don't have much of a relationship and for good reason. He did do some pretty awful things to me and you when you were growing up, but you stopped all that when you got of age. I know he might not be somebody you would've chose to be your father, but he is."

Trying not to bust her bubble but I wanted to really get her attention, so she knew that I wasn't playing about this, I simply asked, "Well, who is Pablo Delgado?"

The glass dropped out of her hand, hitting the floor and breaking into pieces as liquor spilled about. The look on her face was one that I'd never seen before, as her mouth fell open with surprised eyes.

"Pablo Delgado?" she faintly whispered. "Where did you hear that name from?"

"Who is he?" I asked again. I just needed her to come out with the truth. All this beating around the bush was making me impatient.

"Son—"

"Just tell me who he is mama."

"He's someone from my past," she finally said while cleaning the glass off the floor. "Don't walk over here."

"Someone from your past? Someone like the man that's my father?"

"What?! Why would say something like that? Where would you even get such foolishness from?"

"What if I told you that I work with his nephews and they were specifically told by Pablo's brothers to tell me this information?"

She chuckled a little but, deep down, I could tell that she was just trying to process what I'd just said.

"You work with his nephews?" she finally asked. "What kind of work do you do?"

"Mama, come on. You know what I do. You're the one that's always bitchin' about me getting out the game before it's too late."

She continued to clean the glass and liquor up off the floor like she didn't hear me.

"Mama?"

"Son, please, don't do this right now. We already have enough going on."

"When is a good time for us to do this then? So much time has already passed and, from my understanding, Pablo is dead. I think that now is just as good of a time to tell me the truth. Don't you?"

"I don't think now is the time for this conversation, but since you insist. Let's get this over with. I do know Pablo Delgado. He was someone that I was once in love with. We shared something special, but he moved on to be with someone else and I did too. I'm not sure why any of this came up and in saying that you're his son, but you're not. At this point, you're a grown ass man and you've done quite well for yourself without a dad in your life. Jerry was full of shit and, yes, he was abusive. I don't regret one day that you beat his ass and sent him packing. But, the truth is, if Pablo was around, it wouldn't have been much difference. He wouldn't have been present in your life either. The man had way too much shit going on so, if I were you, I'd drop this conversation because that's about all you're going to get out of me," she bluntly acknowledged as she walked out of the kitchen.

I sat stunned that she'd leave me this way, but there was nothing else to say about it. In my mind, she'd said enough. I was already a part of the Delgado empire doing what the other sons were involved in. I also had rank and they treated me as kin so, as far as I was concerned, I would let the situation go for my mother's sake.

I glanced down at my cell phone as it chimed with an incoming text message. I opened the message to see that it was Beans. I simply shook my head because I didn't know what her problem was.

I hope we can sit down as adults and discuss our son. I'm sorry about the way I was acting. I guess it's just my hormones on overdrive. BEANS

I'm actually on my way home now. You can meet me there in about thirty minutes, if that's convenient for you. SMOKE

I'll be there. BEANS

I got up to leave, no longer in the mood for eating after the conversation I'd just had with my mama. I felt drained. My thoughts were all over the place. It was quite a few things I needed to happen in order for me to be okay again and I guess I'd start with Beans.

11

Yazmine "Yaz" Gates

I stood outside of Smoke's crib door, knocking lightly for him to open the door. I know I hadn't called first but, at this stage in our relationship, we did pop-up visits here and there. Plus, we had buried his best friend not long ago and I wanted to make sure that he was good. As I stood there contemplating if I should call him to see where he was at, his aggy ass, big belly baby mama popped up from around the corner. I did everything in my power not to roll my eyes. First thought came to mind was wondering why she was here. She didn't get enough of his attention earlier today. Or maybe that wasn't the kind of time that she really was seeking. To play it off, I smiled at her but could tell the friendly gesture wasn't going to be reciprocated.

"Hey, I just got here and it doesn't seem like Smoke is here yet," I said, still with this fake ass smile plastered across my face.

"Well, he told me to meet him here," she said in the most unbothered way. "He never said that you would be here too."

"He doesn't know that I'm here, yet," I responded.

"Go figure," Beans uttered to my dislike, but I would let her have that.

"You okay?" I pondered. "You seem a bit frustrated or upset. I hope that me being here isn't the cause of this disappointed expression on your face."

"Actually, it is," she blatantly responded. "Rashad and I already have a lot of things we need to discuss. I certainly don't want to do that in front of a third party, regardless of what you are to him."

I grinned under my breath, which was my way of holding my composure before I slapped this pregnant bitch right in that sassy ass mouth of hers. "I don't want to interfere in nothing that you and *Rashad*," I mocked, "have to talk about," I finished with a slick roll of the eyes. "I don't know why you're so upset with me, but there is no need for that. I can leave. I'm not insecure at all, sweetie. Trust me, it's not a problem," I told her.

"Oh, so you think I'm insecure when I'm the one carrying his son?"

"Girl bye. Anybody can carry his seed, but what really matters is the one that's carrying his heart. Is that you?" I sarcastically asked.

"Yooooo, wassup Babe?" Smoke said with that handsome ass smile of his as he walked up. I didn't even see him coming being that I was too distracted giving Beans po' ass the business. "I didn't know you was stopping by."

"Sorry 'bout that. I was trying to surprise you." I smiled. "But, I didn't know that you would already have company, so I'll leave."

"Nonsense," Smoke quickly said, as he looked at Beans. "We can talk up front and she can go in the bedroom until we're done. Cool?"

"Well, I was hoping that it would just be me and you—"

"Like I said, I can leave," I cut in.

"No, you're staying," Smoke said while unlocking the door. "You coming in?" he asked Beans, as I just stood there. "Come on, Babe."

I smiled, taking that as my queue to do as my man had said. Beans frowned with an unpleasant look on his face, as I walked right past her stubborn ass.

"What you gon' do Beans?" he questioned.

"I'm coming, but let's get this shit over with so I can leave."

"Cool," Smoke said with a nod of the head.

"I'm going in the bedroom," I said, as Beans sat down on the sectional couch in the living room. But, first, I stopped by the fridge and grabbed me a Corona to drink. As I headed in the bedroom, I could hear Smoke say, *well this has been way overdue. Let's talk.*

Once in the bedroom, I turned on the TV while fidgeting with my phone in my hand until I decided to give Tam a call. On the first ring, she answered.

"Wassup Sis?"

"Hey girl, you busy?" I asked.

"Nah, I'm just laying my ass across this bed trying to figure out what I'm going to do later tonight. What you doing?"

"Sitting in Smoke's bedroom waiting for him and

Beans to finish their long overdue conversation about that baby."

"Girl, why you ain't ear hustling? You know my nosey ass would be right there being nosey."

I laughed. "I don't wanna hear what that crazy bitch is saying. She already was in her feelings because I was here when she got here."

"Well, the bitch need to get over that."

"My thoughts exactly."

"But, I still think you need to be eavesdropping. Just so you'll be in the know. I mean, she could be talking about you."

"Well, Smoke ain't going to allow that. I know him. Why you think I'm here? Because homegirl wanted me gone and he wasn't with the shits."

"Good for him. I wish Heavy was more like that."

"Girl, I believe Heavy knows what's good for him. Everything he has asked in the little time that y'all have been talking, you've come through. It may not seem like it, but he'll start checking his baby mamas too when they get out of line. He definitely doesn't seem like the type to let none of them get away with nothing he doesn't approve of."

"I can believe it," she agreed. "But, only time will tell. How was the service? I know it was sad."

"Yea, it was pretty sad. The only people I was concerned about was Nova and Smoke. They both held up as good as can be expected."

"Yea, I just hung up with Nova not long ago. She

was at your house packing up some things to bring over here."

"I'm glad she's okay. I think she handled this better than we predicted. You know she's emotional as hell. However, them breaking up already played a big role in that. Honestly, she had already gotten over him," I said, with thoughts of Smoke and Beans talking still lingering in my mind.

"Plus, the way things ended weren't the best."

"I agree."

"All of this helped her be strong. I hate it happened to him, but he'd been asking for this for as long as I've known him," Tam said.

"That's bad to say, but I totally agree. He wasn't a good guy. I mean, I'm sure he may have had his good moments with her, but the dude was a real asshole and super disrespectful."

"I agree. Anyway, may he rest in peace."

"Now Sis, you know he's probably turning up a shot of D'Usse with the—"

Tam bust out laughing. "Don't you say it. We know his ass is burning up right about now."

I laughed back. "I'm just saying. Anyway, my nosey ass is curious about this talk that's going on upfront."

"Go be nosey, damnit." Tam grinned. "You know you want to."

"Nah, I think I'll chill till he comes in here. He'll tell me what they talk about."

"You sholl got a lot of trust in him," Tam eased in.

"Until he does something that makes me feel differently," I responded.

"Well, I guess you're right about that part. For the most part, Smoke is a good one. You should definitely appreciate him."

"Trust me, I do," I said, with a smile on my face. "Hold up, Nova is texting me," I said, now glancing down at the screen of my phone and opening the message. "She wants us to link at y'all's spot tonight. She says that she has something she wants to discuss with me and you."

"I'd been trying to think of something to do, so that sounds good to me."

"I just messaged her back that it's a go. I wonder what she wants to talk about?"

"No telling but I hope it's good."

"Shit, me too," I said, just as my fine ass man appeared in the doorway. "Let me call you back."

"Okay cool," Tam said, as we ended our call.

"You good babe? The talk is over already?"

"Yea, I don't know what's going on with Beans, but she has never acted like this. She's in her feelings because you're here. She barely wanted to talk and, so, we really didn't get anywhere. She left the conversation saying that she'll let me know when she goes into labor and I can either be there or not."

"Damn, she's cold with it."

"Well, I ain't kissing her ass just to be a part of my

son's life. I know that."

"I really didn't want to say anything, but I think you should have a blood test just to make sure he's yours."

"That's funny you would say that because my mom suggested the same thing."

"Oh, did she?" I pondered with surprised eyes.

"Yes, she did and, honestly, I'm contemplating it for the first time. Especially after she has been lying about the possibility of my father being someone else."

"Huh, say what now?" I asked with a frown on my face.

"It's been so much going on that I didn't even want to talk about this but, apparently, my father is someone name Pablo Delgado."

"Delgado?" I questioned, as that last name began to ring a bell. "As in the Delgado's? Rah and them?"

"Yes," he responded with a nod of the head.

I stared at him with squinted eyes. Never had I paid attention to his looks but, come to think about it, he definitely favored them. However, to me, one mixed person always favored another in some form or fashion. Since knowing that Jerry was biracial, I didn't think much of it. I did think Smoke's hair was a lot straighter and silkier when it grew a little length to it. Unlike most other mixed people I knew. Their hair was a lot curlier than his.

"You sure?"

At that time, Smoke pulled out a picture and

handed it to me.

"Wow," I uttered. He definitely looked a lot like this man. I still couldn't believe that I hadn't paid that much attention to his looks compared to that of Rah and Heavy. But, we didn't really hang around them like that. So, I could see how it was easily overlooked. However, now I could see it. "How do you feel about this?"

"I really don't know how I feel about it. I mean this dude is dead so, not only did I not know him, I'll never get to know what kind of man he really was."

"Awww, I'm sorry to hear that."

"No, it's cool babe. I'd made my peace after whooping Jerry's ass and sending him on his way. I'm a grown man now. I'll make my own memories with my own family," he said, causing me to smile inside. I knew his own family included me and that's all that counted. "I'm also thankful that I do know now, and that Rah and the rest of the family already accepts me."

"Well, that's all that matters," I assured him. "So, what are you going to do about this Beans situation? I mean, for y'all to have been such besties at one point, she sure as hell acting funking towards you now."

"And, that's because I've clearly moved on. Apparently, she had feelings of us being together someday, but I never looked at her like that. She was just a really close person to me, someone that I could confide in and get advice."

"Someone you also nailed to the cross when your ass was horny," I added, as he laughed out loud.

"Well, you know."

I grinned. "Yea, I know. That big belly says it all."

"Stop it," Smoke teased, leaning towards me and kissing my lips. Oh, how I just loved the affection and those sweet kisses. He was a stand-up guy and indeed the man I dreamed of marrying one day. "What are your plans this evening?"

"I really wanted to come over and chill with you, but Nova messaged me and wants to link with us at she and Tam's crib tonight. She says she has something she wants to talk to us about."

"Oh, okay. I wonder what that could be?"

"No telling but, of course, I'm going so I can find out."

"As you should," he agreed, as he glanced down at the screen of his cell phone after having received a text message. Quietly, he opened and read it. "Well, looks like I'm invited to the family dinner tonight."

"What family dinner?" I pondered.

"With the Delgado's. Seems I get to finally meet everybody."

"Well, that's a good thing, right?" I asked, since he was looking at me with uncertainty.

"Yea, I guess. Well, yea it is a good thing," he said, now with a bit more confidence. "I want to know these people more. I mean, I already know Rah, Heavy, and Jose. I've even known a few more cousins in the business, but I've never met the old heads, so this should be interesting."

"And, I can't wait to hear all about it," I said, grabbing him softly by the face and kissing him. "You got this Babe, as always. And always, we got each other."

12

Nova Thang

"How are you feeling?" Rah asked.

"I'm feeling pretty good. I'm glad to be back at the crib and unpacking my things. It feels nice to have a place I can call home."

"Even nicer to have a place you can call your own. I told you I would help you take your things over there. One call, that's all," he said, causing me to smile

"I know, but I didn't want to bother you. I know you have that dinner this evening with your family."

"We have that every week for the most part, unless something comes up. But you know I still had time to do that for you."

"I know and I truly appreciate it. However, I'm not a baby."

"But, you're my baby."

I smiled from ear to ear. His ass had me blushing like crazy. "So, are we still linking later tonight?"

"Yea, as long as you've not changed your mind," he responded.

"No, I haven't. I'm gonna have drinks with Tam and Yaz in a couple of hours though. I want to tell them what

I've decided to do with you because I want their support."

"Ain't nothing wrong with that. I was actually hoping you would do that. I don't mind them being a part of the business because I know they'll have your back."

"I appreciate that. I don't know what they're gonna say but, I'm sure once it's all said and done, they'll be down."

"Well, if you need me to explain some things just in case they're unsure, I don't mind."

"I'll explain everything that I know. If it's cool, when you start to train me, I'd like for them to be in on that as well."

"Say less," he said, making me smile. "How is the Koban family?"

"Everybody was surprisingly taking things pretty well. I mean, they were definitely sad and crying, but it wasn't as bad as I thought it would've been. They didn't show his body, only a large photo of him was shown. They played a plethora of short videos of him growing up and pictures of him with family and friends. I must admit, it brought back memories, even though I wasn't on any. I just could remember some of the decent times we had."

"I understand, it does take you back to a time when things were good. It's the same way I felt about my uncle. He was always the fun, loving, joking one of the crew. Always had us laughing, always wanted to take us places with him, always had talks about women with us—"

"Awww, I know you miss him."

"Every day," he said in a gentle tone. "It's been five years, but it feels like yesterday."

"I can only imagine," I responded. I could hear the hurt in his voice. Just that told me a lot about how he viewed family. They meant a lot to him.

"Now, I pray every day that we don't relive that so soon with my brother. We're the only two by my parents, so it's not easy on them. It's crazy how you can have all the money in the world, but sometimes even that can't save a person."

"You said a mouthful then, but I'm praying that he'll be okay."

"Thanks love, me too. We all are."

"Hold on right quick, my brother is calling."

"Ok."

I clicked over. "Wassup Bro?"

"Hey Sis, just wanted to check on you. How are you? I know they buried that nigga today. Mama told me."

"Yea, they did and I'm doing ok. How are you? I haven't heard from your ass. You know Tam is still fussing about her money."

"What money?" CJ asked like he was clueless.

"Boy, don't play with me. You know what damn money."

He grinned in the phone like he was playing with me. "Man, I'm coming home today. I'll talk with her when I get there."

"You better call her first. I'm sure she don't want no more surprise visits from you."

"That woman loves me. It don't matter how I show up," he joked.

"Bitch better have her money," I laughed. "Don't show up without that."

"Man, hush. I'll call you when I get on that end."

"Alright." I grinned. I clicked over to resume my conversation with Raheem. "I'm back."

"Like you never left," he teased.

"Sorry about that. My brother just wanted to check on me. He said he's coming home today."

"He doesn't live here?"

"He lives anywhere he lays his head. However, he's been in Charlotte, North Carolina these past few months."

"Oh ok," Rah responded. "Are y'all tight or close with each other."

"Yea, I love him with all my heart. He just has some slick ways."

"What do you mean by that?"

I sat pondering over if I wanted to answer that. I didn't really want Raheem to know my brother's thieving, manipulative background. They hadn't even met yet. I didn't want to put a bad taste in his mouth already. Besides, I had high hopes that CJ would change. I just hoped that it'd be sooner than later.

"Never mind me," I answered, wanting to move on

to something else. "I think I wanna take a lil nap before Yaz gets here. Tam is in her room running her mouth on the phone. She's probably talking to Heavy. You know she likes him a lot. She just doesn't know how he really feels about her."

"He likes her too. Just don't tell her I told you that."

"I won't," I assured him.

"Go on and take a nap. Just call me later after your girl's night in."

I grinned. "Yep, because my night out doesn't start until I head your way."

"You got that right."

"I'll call you before I leave to head your way," I added. "Enjoy your dinner tonight with the family."

"Thank you and you enjoy as well."

I smiled. "Thank you, I will." After smiling so hard til my jaws began to tingle, I ended the call. Either we'd hang up at the same time, or Rah would wait for me to hang up first. That was another thing I liked about him, such a gentleman on the inside and very thuggish on the outside.

I laid across my comfortable bed with sweet thoughts of Rah and, before I knew it, I'd drifted off to sleep. I woke up a little over an hour later with Yaz screaming in my face.

"WAKE UP BIIIITCH!!"

"Girl gone," I uttered while rubbing my eyes and trying to get my thoughts together.

"You may as well get up. I brought us food from the restaurant. Uncle Chin made sure to pack some of your favorites. He also said he'll stop by tomorrow to see you," Yaz informed me, just as Tam entered my bedroom.

"Bitch, get your ass up!"

I couldn't help but laugh, knowing that any sleep I was still looking forward to getting was over.

"I got us a bottle of Hennessy. Time to get wasted and talk shit," Tam teased.

"Okay, I'm coming," I told them. "Now, get out of here!"

"Don't make me come back with a glass of ice-cold water. I promise I'll drown your ass if you go back to sleep," Yaz clowned.

I sat up on the side of the bed while yawning. "I'm up bitches, I'm up!"

They laughed while walking out the room. I knew I had to get my shit together and join them. Plus, I had some exciting news to discuss, and I couldn't wait to get their input.

We sat Indian style on pillow tops in front of the leather ottoman, which was decorated with boxes of delicious food from Daddy's restaurant. As we sipped our Hennessy and ate the good food, I figured now would be the time to speak about the proposal that I'd said yes to. Before I could even get it out, Tam started.

"Your ugly ass brother called me."

I grinned under my breath. "What he said?"

"He said he was coming by," she responded.

"You letting him come by after what he did the last time?" Yaz asked.

"Bitch better have my money. That's the only reason why I'm letting him stop by."

Yaz and I laughed. "He did call me and said that he was going to be on this end," I commented.

"I have nothing for him, but he better have something for me. I just still can't believe he did me like that, as much as I've looked out for him. He was dead ass wrong for that."

"I agree," I stated.

"I don't know what the hell CJ be thinking about," Yaz said. "I hope he gets his shit together before a nigga fuck around and hurt him. He can't just do shit like that and think it's cool."

"You're right, and I've told him that over and over again," I added.

"I don't have money like that. I don't know what made him think I wouldn't miss that."

"Me either," I said, but thought to use this as my queue to tell them what I'd signed up for. "Well, speaking of money or the lack thereof, I've accepted a proposition that was asked of me."

Yaz frowned. "What kind of proposition?"

"One that could make me, well us, a lot of money," I answered.

"Oh Lordt, not some get rich scheme. I hope your brother ain't behind this," Tam cut in, causing me to laugh.

"I'd be a damn fool to follow CJ's ass up."

"So, it ain't him?" Tam asked.

"Hell nawl," I responded with laughter. "You're the only one that falls for his bullshit."

"I bet that's over and done with," she assured us. "Anyway, what's this get rich scheme?"

"We're going to join Rah's team," I told them like I just knew that they'd be down.

"Say what now?" Yaz quickly intervened. "His team? Like as in what Smoke do?"

"Yes, like as in what Smoke do," I told her.

"Girl stop!" Tam chimed in, as she looked at me with confusion. "Rah wants you in on the family business? Are you serious?"

"Very," I said with a serious smirk on my face.

"Damn, you must've put that WAP on his ass," Tam joked, causing me and Yaz to laugh out loud.

"Well, you knoooow," I sang in a teasing manner.

"Ohhh shit, Stella got her groove back," Yaz laughed.

"No bitch, Nova got her groove back. Get it right," I mocked.

"I like this new Nova and her new attitude because bitch, I never would've thought you'd even entertain something like this. Hell, we talking about you got that WAP, but Rah must have that golden stick," Tam clowned.

"Filled with diamonds," Yaz added.

I simply laughed at them.

"So, are you really going to do this?" Yaz pondered.

"Only if y'all are down to do it with me," I told them.

"Shit, you know I'm down. It ain't like I got a 9 to 5," Tam said.

"Yea, but I do," Yaz cut in. "I can't just stop working at the restaurant to do this."

"I don't expect you to, nor would I ask you to do that. Hell, I'll still be working there too. I know daddy loves to see me on a regular and nothing makes him happier than having me work with him. I just won't be working as many hours. I'm gonna tell him that I'll be getting back in school, but I still want to work there part-time."

"And will you go back to school or is that a lie?"

"I will be going back to school once this money starts rolling in," I assured Yaz.

Yaz smiled. "Good, because I'm going back too. I still aspire to open our pediatric doctor's office someday."

"Me too," I told her. "I know it seemed like I'd gotten lost in Kirk's world, but I'm over that now. I was over it the day I left him. I just had to bounce back. His death was untimely, but he brought all of that on himself. I'm not dwelling on that anymore. I just want to get over it and move forward with my life."

"Spoken like a true survivor," Tam commented.

"I agree," Yaz said while holding up her glass of Hennessy. "Let's toast to that."

We all clinked glasses and turned up our drinks. They didn't know the half of what I'd gone through while dealing with Kirk, but I was definitely grateful that it was over now.

"Speaking of Kirk. How is his family doing?"

"They seemed to be handling it okay, I guess. His mom just seemed out of it for the most part. His dad is definitely the strong one, but even his sister and brother seemed to be doing okay. I gotta be honest though. I'm surprised they didn't press the issue about us being there that morning. It's like they took our word for it and so did the police."

"I'm sure they could tell we had nothing to do with that. Plus, he had no scuffle marks on him. The nigga just ended up in that lake."

"And dead as a doorknob," Tam added.

"Don't say that," Yaz cut in with a shake of the head.

"I'm just saying," Tam said while pouring herself another glass of Hennessy. "I'm sure the police are still investigating, but I'm not sure what they'll end up with."

"Nothing, because to my knowledge and what I learned from his mom, that it's a closed case. They figure he was drunk and went out to the lake and fell in and bumped his head on the way down. He was too drunk to pull himself out."

"Oh wow, but what if that really did happen?" Yaz said.

I shrugged my shoulders. "I really can't remember too much about that night besides the nigga drugging me."

"Damn man, can we please move on from this subject? It's blowing my high," Tam said as she pulled out the edible gummies. "Y'all want some?"

"Damn right," I said, snatching the bag from her.

"A'ight, but don't eat but one. You know you get paranoid if you do too much," Yaz clowned and took the bag from me, so she could eat one too.

"Whatever bitch. I can hold my shit."

"If you say so," she and Tam laughed, as she glanced down at her cell phone.

"That must be Heavy, got you smiling like that," I said with a playful smirk.

"It's CJ and I ain't smiling for his ass. He said he's about to drop my money off. That's what the hell I'm smiling about."

"Yea, yea," I teased. "So, wassup? Y'all gonna do this with me or nah?"

"Shit, I'm in," Tam quickly answered, followed by Yaz.

"When we start?"

"Shit, as soon as Rah gives me the word. I'll be going over tonight, so I'll know more by tomorrow. I did ask him if he would school me along with y'all, so everybody is on the same page."

"And?" Tam pondered.

"And it's a go," I responded. Everybody smiled with Hennessy on our breaths and dollar signs in our eyes. We were all ready to make some money. I looked at this as an opportunity of a lifetime. I just hoped that it wouldn't lead to mo' money, mo' problems.

13

Mrs. Koban

"I see you're finally up," Mr. Koban said as he entered the bedroom with a cup of coffee in his hand.

"Thanks Darling," I said, appreciating the hot coffee that he had made for me. I felt worn out and still tired from everything that had been going on. Burying Kirk yesterday had me down and out. Never did I think I'd be the one in this unbearable situation. It was so much going on that I felt like I was starting to lose control. That was hard to admit, being that I was the queen of control. I ruled everything around me, including my family. However, for once, I felt defeated and it was nothing I could do about it. This feeling was totally out of my control and I didn't know what to do.

"You okay, my love?"

"No," I somberly responded while sipping from my hot coffee. "I'm saddened by the events that have taken place. I'm still trying to process it all, but it's the hardest thing in the world to grasp."

"I know the feeling."

"What are we going to do? Are we supposed to let this case close? I mean, could he really have been that intoxicated that he fell in the lake and drowned like they said he did?"

"My thing is that the home footage that we expected to see wasn't even working. So, we don't know what happened. It was nothing there. That was our way of figuring this out or even seeing if there was any foul play."

"I know," I said. "I still can't believe he left that condo to Nova. Can you believe it?"

"No, I didn't even know he owned it. He was really making a lot of money."

"Illegally," I pointed out. "Which could've had a lot to do with what happened to him."

"He should've known the consequences."

"I agree, and I kept trying to tell him to get a legitimate job."

"He wasn't coming around us like that and, when he did, he was very standoffish. Kind of isolated himself from the family, and that bothered me. However, I do feel like he has always missed something in his life," he said, now staring over at me.

"Please, don't start that right now."

"It's the truth. You dove into your work and forgot about him."

"I never forgot about my child. I love him with every being in me."

"I'm not saying that you didn't but, under the circumstances, you should've showed him more attention and love. I do believe that was one of the main reasons he turned out the way he did."

At that moment, I'd gotten pissed off. I stood up and headed in the bathroom to dash a bit of cold water on my face. I felt like he was really trying me at a time when it wasn't cool to try me.

"Don't get mad Darling. I'm just saying," he added. "I know it's a touchy subject for you, but you've never wanted to deal with it head on, especially after the fact."

I was about to burst with emotions, but I held it in and dashed the cold water on my face then glanced in the mirror at myself. It was rather hard to even look at the person that was staring back at me and listening to my husband with this bullshit only made it worse.

"I wanted us to go to counseling, but you were too good for that."

"I did let Kirk go to counseling. I was the one that felt that he should go."

"I'm not talking about Kirk," he barked, now like he was the one with an attitude. "I'm talking about us."

"Counseling wouldn't have done anything for us. We made a decision and stuck with it. Now, that's something I have to live with for the rest of my life."

"Oh, do you think you're the only one that has to live with that decision? You can't be serious right now."

"Don't fucking start with me! It was mainly your decision!"

"No, it wasn't!" he argued back. The tone of his voice was definitely one that I hadn't heard in a long, long time. So, to hear it now told me that this shit had gotten about as real as it ever had. I didn't know if it was because we'd swept things under the rug for as long as we could, but it was definitely coming to surface to now. "It was your decision when you fucked up!"

"What?! So, we're going to do this now? Now? Out of all times, now?"

"Why not?! We haven't done it before."

"We went through this shit already, thirty fucking years ago."

"No, you went through it and then filled me in after the fact!" he scolded me. "In other words, you wouldn't have said nothing had you not been threatened to come clean."

"Please Philip. I'm not in the mood for this," I responded, now getting an instant headache.

"Me either, but I feel like Kirk is gone because you weren't honest with him."

"Well, what about you? You could've been honest with him too but you played just as big a part in this as I did."

"I don't see it that way. Everything was your decision and, then, you told me what you wanted to do. I don't know if you felt that made things easier on us, but I could never get over it."

"Wish I would've known that a whole lot sooner than now," I spat with a roll of the eyes.

"You knew my feelings on this situation. You knew how I felt, so don't act like me speaking on this is all new to you."

The whole time I'd been standing in the bathroom going back and forth with my husband. He wanted to bring up my past, and I just wanted to crawl back in bed and grieve peacefully. I knew I'd made some horrible decisions in life and I wasn't proud of nothing that had happened. I too had to live with this shit every fucking day, so for him to be throwing it up in my face now was wrong on his part. He knew I was hurting, yet he was pointing the finger like this was all my fault.

I raised Kirk the best I knew how. He didn't lack or slack for nothing. I may not have been as present as he wanted me to be, but I was still dealing with my own emotional trauma. Sleeping with a married man thirty years prior brought on a lot of consequences. One that led to an unexpected pregnancy. If his wife hadn't found out about our affair and threatened to expose me, all would've been fine. I probably could've gotten away with it without Philip ever knowing about it. But that wasn't the case, and I had to be honest with him. Did it help that the man I slept with was also a doctor that worked in the same hospital as me? Hell no, it only made matters worse and it took Philip a long time to get over it. From the looks of things, he still hadn't fully gotten over it. He wants to sit here and point fingers at me, but he too was the blame. He could've stood up and said something, but us making that decision without him was probably the best outcome for him. Being that he didn't have to deal with the problem himself, nor would it linger over his head like it'd been lingering over mine.

I dried my tears, trying to compose myself and simply walked out of the bedroom. I didn't want to keep talking about something that had already happened. What was done was done and I was over it. Once downstairs, I headed straight into the kitchen and fixed myself a mimosa with a splash of tequila. I just wanted to ease my thoughts the best way I knew how. The doorbell rang, causing me to frown. Like, who could be showing up at my house eight o'clock in the morning? I knew it wasn't my Phil or Nessa. They weren't coming back over until later this evening. I definitely wasn't up for any company, so I was glad to hear Philip come down the stairs, calling out that he'd get it. I stood in silence as I listened to hear who it was.

Once the door opened, Philip said, "Wow, I'm almost at a loss of words. Thanks for coming."

I frowned while thinking to myself, *Who the hell is he talking to?*

"Thank you, sir. I'm glad you called," the deep voice said. "How are you?"

"I'm hanging in there," Philip answered. "How are you? How was that long drive?"

"The drive here gave me a lot of time to think. I still don't know how I feel, but I'm okay. I'd been waiting at the hotel for a few days now. I didn't think you were going to invite me over."

"I know and I'm sorry about that. We've just had a lot going on."

"I understand. I hate I couldn't fully be a part of this. But, it's so much I need to know."

"I know, and there is no better time than now," Philip said and then called out to me.

I stood frozen like I couldn't move. My gut was screaming on the inside that this was finally happening, but I wasn't ready. I wasn't even given the courtesy by my husband to even allow this right now. What the hell was he thinking?

"Darling, please come here!" Philip called out again.

I sat my glass down on the kitchen countertop, feeling nervous as hell inside. I really wanted to dash out the back door and not look back, but hearing him call me again made me realize that I had to face my past in order to get through my present. I nervously walked in the living room that led to the foyer area and, the minute I bent the corner, the presence that stood before me was something I don't think I ever could've prepared myself for. With my eyes wide open and my whole body full of shock, things quickly became fuzzy as I blacked out.

14

Nova Thang

It had been a month since the death of Kirk and things for me was actually looking up. I know that may have sounded somewhat mean or uncaring, but it was the truth. I still had my moments in thinking about us and, even though I wished it could've been nothing but of the good times, I was always reminded that they weren't always good. The best thing that could've come from me dealing with Kirk was being introduced to Rah. Even though it wasn't exactly by Kirk, he still made our connection easier.

I smiled at the thought of picking up my first drop later today. Rah had already taught me, Tam, and Yaz the ropes with Heavy, Jose and, of course, Smoke included. Without a doubt, I knew they had our fronts and backs and would always make sure that nothing happened to us. I'd met my crew and, from the looks of things, they already had mad respect for me and my girls. Well, except for this one dude that didn't seem too thrilled to be answering to a woman, but I didn't care about him. As long as he didn't fuck with my grind, then I was good. I was only there to collect for the most part, to oversee that the product was available, and to make sure that everything was good. Nothing or nobody was going to stop that.

"Why you ain't on the clock?" Cheryl asked me with her hands propped on her hips.

This bitch, I mumbled, with a slick roll of the eyes.

"You've been sitting here forever, and we have a lot of tables that need to be served," she added. "You don't even have on your uniform."

I shook my head because this bitch was always determined to take me out of my character. "I don't have on my uniform because I'm off today. I'm only here to speak with Yaz once she gets a break. I don't know what your problem is with me, but you really need to tame that stank ass attitude of yours," I told her as politely as I could.

"I saw your name on the schedule," Cheryl continued, as I stood to my feet. I clearly was about tired of her.

"Well, go look again because my name isn't on the schedule."

"I sure will," she sassed but, before she could walk off, she started again. "It's because of you that Kirk is dead."

I frowned. Was this bitch really doing this right here, right now? At this point, I was pissed, but the last place I wanted to show my ass was at my father's restaurant. That was the only reason I'd spared this bitch for so long. I glanced around, noticing that it was only us in the waiting area, which was a good thing because I was about to give this hoe the business. "I know you were fucking Kirk. You ain't nothing but a snake ass hoe. You're always fucking somebody that clearly doesn't want nothing but that lil tainted ass pussy. Because from what I'm told, everybody knew that Kirk didn't want you either."

"Tainted? Bitch, you crazy if you think this pussy is tainted. Why you think everybody wants it then?"

"Because it's easy, bitch," I shot back, just as Yaz intervened out of nowhere.

"Whoa, aye, don't do this here," she said, stepping in-between us. "What's wrong with y'all? Uncle Chin is in the kitchen. What you think he would've said if he walked up instead of me?"

"Your cousin the one started," Cheryl said.

I rolled my eyes, wanting to slap the bitch.

"That's hard to believe Cheryl," Yaz responded, coming to my defense. She already knew that Cheryl hated my guts. She also knew that I'd done everything I could to avoid the drama with her ass. "If you don't get yo' ass back to work right now, I'll make sure that you're fired today."

"Oh, you're going to fire me, but Nova is on the schedule to work today but she ain't even working."

"Nova is not on the schedule today."

"I tried to tell her that."

"She's on the schedule for tomorrow. Did you check good or were you just trying to start some shit?"

Cheryl looked at me with fury in her eyes. I knew the bitch wanted all the smoke, but I wasn't with it. However, when the time was right, I was going to do her ass, she could best believe that. Without saying another word, she walked off. She knew she couldn't afford losing this job. After all, the tips were the best and she wouldn't find another place that was going to pay her non-educated ass this good.

"I'm so sick of her," I said, the minute she was gone.

"I know." Yaz nodded. "I thought y'all bitches was about to fight. I could see you had gotten in her face. That's why I hurried over. Thank God wasn't nobody really paying attention. Come on, let's walk out front."

The minute we stepped outside, I looked over at her with a huge smile on my face. "So, you ready bitch?!"

Yaz laughed. "Calm down bitch," she teased. "Of course, I'm ready."

"I'm just so excited."

"I see. Honestly, I can't wait to clock out. This is going to be interesting. I feel like we're going to be the next Queen Pens in the game."

"I know right," I enthusiastically agreed.

"So, this evening we're doing the whole shebang, right? We'll be—" she started but paused as a few people walked up to enter the restaurant. Once they were inside, she continued, "we'll be checking the inventory and picking up the drop, is that right?"

"Yep," I responded. "I'll also talk with the Monk about the supply and to make sure that the his runners are on point. You know that's mandatory and something that I'll need to report back to Rah."

"I don't like his lil funky ass attitude," Yaz pointed out.

"I don't either. Everybody else seems to be cool

with me stepping in and being a top runner—"

"Everybody but him," Yaz intervened.

"I think it's because I'm a woman. Plus, I'm sure he felt like he should've been next in line, yet Rah chose me instead. Not only that, I know talk has gone around that I was once Kirk's lady."

"Ole talking ass maggots, but they better not talk too loud or Rah will have their heads served on a silver platter."

I grinned with a nod of the head. "You know what to say."

"Anyway, I'm coming over as soon as I get off. I know Tam ass is ready."

"You already know it. That's all she's been talking about. I left her and Heavy at the house. That's the real reason why I came by here. I just wanted to pass the time."

"Her and Heavy getting real heavy."

"Same thing I said," I agreed. "I'm just really glad she's found someone that seems just as interested in her as she do in him."

"Yea because I never thought she'd get over CJ."

"Shit, she ain't stun his ass now. He's been trying to get over there since he moved back here, but she ain't having it."

"I see he's been having a lot of money lately. Even auntie was talking about it the other day. I hope he ain't did no crooked shit to get it."

"I hate to even think about it."

"That's why he's back," Yaz stated. "You know how he do."

"Trust me, I know. Hopefully, he'll do right this time and get his shit together."

"Who knows?" Yaz commented. "Anyway, let me get back to work. I'll see you later."

"Okay," I said, as she walked back in the restaurant and I headed for my ride. I looked back more than a few times because I felt like a bitch was watching me. Once in my car, I glanced around the crowded parking lot. There were people going in and out of the restaurant. Nothing looked unusual, so I shrugged it off, started my engine and headed back to the crib.

About thirty minutes later, I pulled up to my condo. I was still in shock that it was actually mine. Kirk probably didn't mean to leave this to me, but I was grateful that he did. I sat in the car for a few minutes, just soaking it all up. I don't know why, but this had become routine every time I'd park. As I sat there, this black Hellcat Charger circled the block at least two times. It should've been something that I overlooked, but I couldn't. If I wasn't mistaken, I believe I saw that same car parked at the restaurant. After it disappeared again, I instantly jumped out the car and went straight into my crib. An uneasy feeling was taking over.

Once inside, I called out to Tam, but she didn't answer. I checked the front area and went into her bedroom to see that she had left. I knew she wouldn't be gone too long because we had business to take care and she definitely didn't want to miss out on that. As I made my way back up front to dig my cell phone out of my purse to call her, the doorbell rang. I frowned, not knowing who that could be. Tam and Yaz had a key. It could've been CJ though, since he was back.

"Who is it?" I called out while making my way to the door.

"Kobe," the deep voice responded.

"Kobe," I softly repeated, almost in a whisper. I didn't know a Kobe, but I opened the door anyway. My heart began to race, as I stared at the man standing before me. The unexpected, yet somewhat familiar face to face encounter was too much for me to handle and, before I knew it, I blacked out.

****

"Hey, get up. You okay?"

I could faintly hear a man's voice in my ear, as I slowly began to regain consciousness. I woke up as my eyes stretched wide open. The guy staring back at me looked so much like Kirk, but I knew that Kirk was dead.

"What the fuck?" I groggily said, trying to sit up.

"No, just lay back and chill out for a second," he said, as I noticed that I was now lying on the sectional in my entertainment room. "I'm sorry that I startled you, but I just had to meet you."

"This gotta be a dream," I let out while trying to sit up. What the hell was going on? "Please, talk. What's going on? Who are you?"

"I'm Kirk's twin brother."

My eyes stretched and so did my mouth. "His brother?! His twin brother?!"

"Yes, I know you didn't know anything about me, and for good reason, I guess," he said, "but let me explain. "Up until a little over a month ago, I didn't know I was a twin, let alone had a brother that I shared a womb with."

"What do you mean?"

"My biological mother is Julia Koban—"

"What?! None of this is making sense to me."

"I know, so you're only experiencing half of what I was feeling when I found out. I've always thought my mom to be Marissa Stewart."

I frowned. "Who is that?"

"My father's wife of thirty-two years."

"I'm so fucking confused," I let out before I knew it while rubbing in my head. This shit had me baffled like a muthafucka.

"So, let's start from the beginning. I guess from when this crazy shit all started," he said, but all I could do was focus on the fact that he looked so much like Kirk. The shit was scary as hell, to be honest. I felt like I was in the company of a ghost. Not only was it weird, but I was uncomfortable and really wanted him to leave.

"I don't know if I can take this," I told him. "I don't understand why it was a must that you meet me."

"Because you're the only person that I felt knew the real Kirk, my twin brother, and I wanted to learn some things about him. I'm still lost and confused. This is hard as hell for me too. I was living my own life, a good life at that. I'm a surgical doctor and I love what I do, but I can't even get my mind in the right space to even trust that I can do my job the way my patients need me to."

"Wow, you're a doctor too. Just like Mrs. Koban—"

"And, my father," he said.

"So, the Kobans gave you up for adoption?"

"I wouldn't say that because Mr. Koban isn't my father."

"I don't understand," I said with a shake of the head. This shit had gotten even more confusing.

"My father is the Dr. Kobe Stewart. I say that because he's a prominent, well respected, the wealthiest surgeon in the region. When he lived here, he and Mrs. Koban had an affair. They both cheated on their spouses. My mom found out and threatened Mrs. Koban, who then told her husband. Later, she found out that she was pregnant and, to her surprise, it was with twins. I know this is going to sound even stranger, but both men wanted paternity test done. Kirk and I were definitely twins but had different fathers. Mrs. Koban and my father talked and decided that I would go with my father, and Kirk stayed with his biological parents."

"WOW, this is the craziest shit I've ever heard."

"I knew of it being that I'm a doctor, but I didn't know I was a part of something like that."

"I know you must feel out of place," I told him, now feeling kind of sorry for him.

"I found out when Kirk died. Honestly, I wish I hadn't known, but I do and it hurts to know I had a twin brother that everybody kept from me because of their dishonesty in this whole cheating scandal. My dad took me in, and my mom chose to raise me as her own and that's the only life I've ever known. I have two other brothers and two sisters by my parents, but to have missed out on a bond with my twin brother bothers me."

"I'm sure," I said, still trying to comprehend all the crazy shit that he was telling me. "This is wild to me. I don't even know what to say."

"Join the club," Kobe said. "I don't want to hold you any longer. Again, I'm sorry about the way I just showed up here."

"Yea, feels like some stalkerish shit."

"I know and I feel bad about that because I'm far from a stalker, but I saw your name in his obituary and then I saw you at the church. You seemed like the type that would be honest with me and I just want to know more about my brother. What better way to find out than to talk with the woman he spent the last four years with?"

"I understand," I said, standing to my feet.

"If it's cool, I'd like to call you sometimes."

"Sure, that's cool," I said. Within the next few minutes, I had given him my number and had gotten his. He did as he said and left just as quickly as he came. I sat back down with all types of thoughts running through my mind. I almost couldn't catch my breath, but Tam walked through the door and made me remember that I had a job to do. I had to shake this shit, so I could get it done. But later, I'd revisit this shit again and explain to

Tam and Yaz what the fuck had just happened.

****

Once back in the car, I glanced over at Yaz, who was sitting on the passenger side while Tam rode in the back-seat. "How was I?" I pondered, trying to get their take on how we'd just handled our business.

"I think you were great," Yaz answered.

"Yessss bitch, you went in there and handled business. We walked out with over one-hundred and fifty thousand dollars in a fucking duffle bag like bosses."

"We did that! It felt good just to be standing there with y'all, looking at these niggas like, WHAT?!" Yaz exclaimed, as me and Tam laughed out loud.

"I feel like we're going to have some trouble out of that cat name Monk. He seems real life big mad at us. The way he was short talking you and walking around like a spoiled brat that couldn't have his way was pissing me off. Like, nigga, do you know who the fuck you're talking to like that?" Tam said.

"Exactly," Yaz agreed. "I peeped that shit from the minute we stepped inside his quarters. Wasn't we just talking about his bitch ass earlier today?"

"Yep," I answered. "And I peeped it too. That nigga is really in his feelings. I wasn't going to even say nothing because I feel like we can handle our own, but maybe I need to tell Rah about his ass."

"Yea, if I was you, I'd mention it, but don't make a big deal out of it. You don't want him to think you're scared or that you can't handle this position," Tam said.

"I agree," Yaz concurred.

"Y'all are right," I said, looking in my rearview to see Smoke following closely behind us. "So, how long do you think we'll have chaperones?"

"Probably foreeevveerr," Tam joked in Cardi B's voice. "Carrying around this much cash requires a chaperone and I ain't mad about it."

"Me either," Yaz chimed in. "Plus, I loved having my baby on the scene tonight, even though he stayed in his car and watched out from afar."

"Definitely made me feel safer," I agreed with a nod of the head. "They are so professional with it. Even during training, it's like they turn into different men—"

"Fucking savages," Yaz chimed in.

"Hell yea, they're definitely about their business —"

"You can tell from the minute they enter the spot that the respect is real," Tam cut in. "What them niggas say goes."

"You got that right," I assented.

As we rode out to Rah's house, I decided that it was past time to tell the ladies about my unexpected, most shocking visitor earlier. "I didn't want to say nothing, at least not before we picked up our first drop. I really just wanted to stay focused on the situation at hand, but I got some craaaaazzzy shit to tell y'all."

"What?" they damn near asked in unison.

"Fasten y'all's seatbelts because this is about to be an unbelievable, wild ass ride. Shit, I'm still stuck on it, but here goes."

15

Raheem "Rah" Delgado

Me, Heavy, and Jose played pool while waiting for the money to arrive. I was a bit giddy inside just knowing that Nova and the crew had handled their business like we had taught them to. Of course, Smoke had called to give me an update and they passed with flying colors. I knew Nova could do it. Plus, she was eager as hell about it. After beating their ass for the umpteenth time, the fellas were done playing with me. Heavy headed over to the bar to fix another drink, as Jose continued to sip on his Corona.

"So, do you really think that Nova is cut out for this?" Jose asked.

"Shit, I believe she is, but only time will tell," I responded.

"Well, I know Tam is cut out for it. She ain't nothing but a lil gangster in the making. Shawty be down for anything," Heavy said.

"I already know. She's like a reflection of you, to be honest," I teased but was definitely serious.

"I said the same thing." Jose grinned. "Shawty 'bout dat life. I believe if them niggas ever get wrong, she'll be the first to pop one."

"I know right. That's why I got them going to the gun range. They'll be strapped up soon," I said.

Heavy nodded his head to agree. "And, with good reason. You can't really trust niggas these days. They need heat on them at all times."

"I don't know about Smoke's girl. She's down, but she just don't seem like she'll stay in the game too long," Jose said.

"Yea, she's the calmer one. Nova is sweet too, but I can tell she has a feisty side. She just hides it well," Heavy chimed in.

"I can agree with that. But, honestly, none of them will stay in the game long. I don't believe so. I mean, I wouldn't even want them to. I just wanted to see if they would and could. My thing was to show Nova what the business is about, so she'll have the insight on what it is that we do. The more she knows when it comes to me, the more I can see if she's in for the long haul or just here for the time being."

"I feel you, which brings me back to Ginger. She hauled ass on you, but now she suddenly shows back up. What the hell did she want today when she called you?"

"Ironically, she said she was calling to see how I was doing and that she was moving back to town."

"Meaning moving back here?" Heavy asked.

"Well, not here exactly, but I guess back in the city," I explained.

"So, how was that conversation? I know it seemed awkward. You haven't talked to her ass in years."

"I ain't gon' lie, I was shocked to hear her voice. At first, she apologized over and over again for the way she left. She seemed sincere. Plus, I could understand why. I just didn't like the way she moved. We could've talked about it, but I guess it boiled down to her seeing me kill a bitch and that scared her. She even mentioned after seeing that a part of her had gotten scared of me."

"Damn, shit was serious if she felt that way," Jose concluded.

"Yea, it was serious because I didn't know she felt that way, but I would've never hurt her."

"We know that," Heavy said. "She just couldn't handle your lifestyle."

"Just for the hell of it, I engaged in conversation, but it wasn't like that. I believe she wanted to fuck."

"Why you say that?" Jose asked.

"Because while we're talking, she sends over this text message," I said, scrolling through my phone to locate the text. Then, I handed it to Jose, so he and Heavy could read it.

I enjoyed you this morning. You still know how to lay it down. The way you ate my pussy like it was the last meal and tongue fucked me until I was damn near insane in the membrane was no joke. Lol Nah, but seriously the best part was sucking your dick as it slid down my throat. You know that big shit have me gagging. Almost caused me to throw up, but your nasty ass would've loved that. Lol Let's talk about how you fucked and made love to me at the same time. You still got my pussy calling your name. Can't nobody beat it up like you. You are and will always be the man for me. I know shit haven't always been peaches and cream, but I'm glad we're back on one accord. Thanks for showing me you still care and for that I want you to know that I'm not going nowhere. Now, come eat this pussy again. You know I love that shit! Lol GINGER

"What the hell? You fucked her?" Jose asked with a clueless expression.

"Damn, that's what you should've started with. You ain't say all that," Heavy added with a scowl on his face.

"I ain't say all that because ain't none of that shit happen. She copied and resent me an old message. I guess she was trying to spark some flames, but I really didn't feed into it. I did grab my dick because it definitely brought back memories. I ain't let her ass know that though."

Jose and Heavy laughed.

"Hell, I grabbed my dick just reading it," Heavy joked. "Her ass was definitely horny, or she wouldn't have sent no shit like that. I'm surprised she still had messages like that. That shit gotta be old as fuck."

"Let me find out she walking round with the same fucking phone from back then. Bitch ain't heard of an upgrade?" Jose joked.

Heavy and I laughed out loud.

"Apparently not," I responded. "She want us to link up, but I don't want no parts of her. I'm good. She moved on and so did I," I told them.

"That's the spirit," Jose teased.

"I ain't gon' lie. I had mad love for her at one point, but now I feel nothing. I wish nothing but good things for her, but she's definitely not the one for me."

"I totally understand. That's the same way I feel about my baby mama. We have a three-year-old daughter, that's it. I'll always make sure she's good but she's definitely not the one for me. My other baby mamas get that, but she don't."

Jose looked at Heavy with a frown on his face. "If you stop dicking her down, you wouldn't have to worry about her feelings being tied up in you."

I laughed out loud. "He got a point." I nodded.

"She got some good pussy though." Heavy grinned.

"A'ight, that good pussy gon' get you fucked up," I joked.

"I know, that's why I gotta leave her crazy ass alone. Now, she's acting out and don't want me to see my daughter. Like, come on man, it ain't that serious."

"She'll come around," I told him. "Stop giving her ass money and shit and watch how fast she start acting right."

"That part." Jose grinned as he drank his beer.

My phone chirped, indicating that I had a text message. I glanced down at the display screen to see that it was Smoke. "They're about ten minutes away."

"That's wassup," Heavy said. "A smooth run is what I call that."

"Exactly," Jose chimed in. "So, when Nova gets here, are you going to tell her that your ex hit you up?"

"Nigga, what kind of question is that. Hell nawl," I responded. "Why would I do that when I don't even want her ass?"

Heavy laughed. "That's right. Never tell on yourself, whether you want her ass or not."

"I was just joking. Shit, I knew you weren't gonna tell her," Jose laughed.

At that time, my cell phone rang, interrupting our entertainment. Instantly, I answered, when I noticed it was a guard at the front gate.

"Yea."

"Nova, her friends, and Smoke are here," the guard said.

"Let 'em in," I responded.

"Got'cha boss."

"They're here," I said to the fellas.

"The drops have been a lil short since Kirk died."

I nodded my head. "I've peeped that, but I'm on it. It hasn't been by a whole lot but it's noticeable. That's a pretty tight knit crew over there. They stick together, even though they hated Kirk for some reason."

"For good reason," Jose agreed.

"We'll keep an eye on 'em. Maybe they're just adjusting. It's only been a few weeks."

"That's true," Heavy said, just as a knock tapped lightly on my front door, followed by the ringing of the doorbell.

"Come in," I called out. "Wassup ladies?" I said, the

minute Nova, Tam and Yaz entered my house. As they spoke, Nova headed straight over to me for a hug.

"Wassup Handsome?" she said with a big smile on her face.

"Everything is great," I responded. "How was y'all's run?"

"It went exceptionally well," she responded, just as Smoke entered the house carrying the duffle bag full of money. "It's all there," she added, glancing back at the bag.

"Y'all did the damn thang," Heavy chimed in with an approving smile on his face, as he kissed Tam on the lips. "I'm proud of you, baby."

"Thanks baby," she said back.

"We're proud of all of you," Smoke added. "You should've seen 'em walking out—"

"Like some boss bitches," Yaz teased. "It felt like I was in a Scarface movie or something."

We all laughed because I was sure they felt like the mafia with high rank and authority. It felt good to have Nova be a part of the family business. She seemed to be all in, and I liked that about her.

"Y'all want something to drink?" Jose asked, as he headed over to the bar to grab another beer.

"Yea," they all said in unison.

"I want Henny and Stella Rosa mixed," Yaz responded, as she winked at Smoke. I pretty much figured what that look meant.

"I'll have the same," Nova said.

"Me too," Tam slid in.

"How was the drop?" I pondered.

"It was on point tonight," Nova responded.

"That's good. We were just talking about that," Heavy said.

"I appreciate y'all doing this. Thanks Smoke for having their backs."

Smoke nodded his head. That was his way of letting us know that he'd always have our backs. "Family first," he responded.

I poured the cash out of the duffle bag onto the pool table and gave the ladies seven thousand a piece. From the smiles on their faces, they acted like they'd hit the lottery.

"Shiiiit, when is the next drop?" Tam teased.

"In a week." I grinned.

"We'll be there," Yaz chimed in.

We laughed about it, then started small talk. As always clowning around with each other, enjoying the ladies company until Keisha showed up banging on my door.

"Open this damn door!" she yelled out.

"What the fuck? Is that—"

"Yep, your crazy ass baby mama." Heavy sighed with a shake of the head.

"Come in!" I called out. From the sound of her

voice, I knew she wanted all the smoke. "What you did, cuz?"

"Nothing." Jose shrugged, as Keisha entered the house.

"Hey y'all," She spoke and then addressed me. "Rah, you know I'm not here to disrespect your house, so please forgive me. Yo' cousin just keeps trying me."

Before I could say anything, she turned towards Jose and snapped.

"Why the fuck you ain't answering yo' damn phone?! I told you I was going out with my sister for her birthday tonight and I needed you to watch the kids! That's all I asked yo' ass to do and you can't even do that! You over here shootin' the shit, instead of being at home tending to your chirren," she fussed, sounding all ghetto and shit. I still didn't know what he saw in her crazy ass. She must've had the best pussy in town.

"Man, don't bring that dumb shit over here. Yo' stupid ass," Jose fussed back. "I said I was coming, don't fucking rush me!"

"Stupid?! Nigga, I got yo' stupid!"

"Don't see I'm over here handling business?" he said, looking towards the cash on the pool table.

"All I see is yo' ass over here entertaining er'body but ya damn chirren!" Keisha argued back.

"Take yo' ass home before I make you shame!"

"Make me shame!" she sassed but, the minute Jose started towards her, she changed her tune. "That's okay. Stay here! I'm taking the kids to my mama's house and I won't be back tonight!"

"Gon' to ya mama house. Like I give a damn, and stay out all you want but just know you won't be allowed back on this property."

"Like I give a fuck! I don't wanna be out here no more anyway. I'd rather be around my own family."

"Go live yo' ratchet, broke ass life. That's all yo' dumb ass used to anyway. Now, get the fuck on!"

"With pleasure ol' stupid ass nigga," she concluded and, with that, she stormed out of the house. The second the door closed behind her, we bust out laughing.

"Man, I don't know how you deal with her," Heavy said.

I simply shook my head.

"I ain't dealing with shit. Let her dumb ass go. If she wanna move back in the projects with her mama, I really don't give a fuck," he said, now fixing him a straight shot of Henny. Guess she had really struck a nerve because he was chilling for the most part. I assume that was because he really was going to leave early to watch the kids. However, Keisha didn't give the man time to get home.

"You know yo' ass gon' be parked out front of her mama apartment begging her ass back," Heavy joked, as we laughed.

"Shittn' me," Jose responded.

"Well, since the drama has already kicked off. I guess it's a good time to tell y'all what happened to me earlier today."

I looked over at Nova with puzzled eyes. I had

talked to her throughout the day and she hadn't mentioned nothing unusual to me.

"Kirk has a twin brother name Kobe and he showed up at my crib today," she said.

"A twin brother?" I quickly responded. "Why you didn't tell me this earlier?"

"Because I didn't want to be distracted before my first run."

"A twin brother?" Jose repeated with widened eyes.

"What the hell made him show up at your house?" I pondered.

"An even better question is where the hell this nigga been all this time?" Smoke asked. "Kirk never said nothing about having a brother other than Phillip."

"That's because Kirk didn't know. From my understanding, nobody knew except Mr. and Mrs. Koban and Kobe's biological father."

"This shit ain't making no sense," Heavy uttered.

"Just wait, it gets better," Tam slid in.

"See, Mrs. Koban had an affair on Mr. Koban with one of the doctors she worked with. She eventually had to fess up being that her secret had been exposed. Both men wanted a paternity test and, since she was pregnant with twins, it turned out that one belonged to Mr. Koban."

"Kirk," Yaz explained.

"And the other belonged to the other man."

"Kobe," Yaz said.

"Wow, this shit crazy," Jose let out.

"Anyway, the other man took Kobe at birth. His wife agreed to help raise him as her own and Mr. and Mrs. Koban took Kirk."

"So, what would make him pop up now after all these years?" I pondered.

"From what I'm told, Mr. Koban called him after Kirk died because he felt that he had a right to know about his twin brother. That news brought him to town."

"This is some strange shit," Smoke uttered.

"So, he came to you for what?" I asked.

"He wants to know more about his brother. He said he was at the church and that's when he saw me. From looking at the obituary, he saw that I was Kirk's woman."

"Ex woman," I mumbled.

"Well, he said that I looked like someone that would be honest with him about Kirk. Apparently, he doesn't feel like nobody else will keep it one-hundred with him."

"He could've went to Smoke," I said, but then had to catch myself. Clearly, I was in my feelings about this nigga showing up out the blue and running to Nova for answers.

"He did leave but we exchanged numbers. I agreed to tell him anything he wanted to know about his brother."

I stood there not knowing how to feel about them

exchanging numbers, but it was nothing I could say. She was a grown woman and could very well talk to whoever she wanted to, whether I liked it or not.

Jose sat in silence like he was dwelling over what had been said. "That explains why I thought I saw that nigga after he had died."

"You damn sholl said that," Heavy stated.

"They do look just alike. I mean, I could tell the differences but, if you didn't know any better, he could fool you," she said. "I ain't gon' lie, he scared the shit outta me."

"I would've probably fainted too," Tam commented.

"You fainted?" I asked.

"Yea, but he was there to make sure I was okay when I regained consciousness."

"This night can't get any crazier," Jose said, just as Smoke's cell phone began to ring. All eyes immediately set on him.

"Yea," he answered. "Calm down. I'm on the way."

"What happened?" I asked with curious eyes.

"Beans just had the baby," he responded.

"Damn, she been carrying that baby for a long time," Jose teased.

"She was a week overdue," Smoke said. "But, I gotta go. I'll call you later." He kissed an unhappy Yaz on the lips and briskly left.

I just stood in silence, still caught up on what Nova

had just said. Knowing that Kirk had a twin brother didn't sit right with me. Hopefully, he would stay where the fuck he was at because if he caused any trouble for me or Nova, he would be joining his brother, and I meant that.

16

Rashad "Smoke" Rivers

I pulled up to Nova's house with a smile on my face. It was good to see that Yaz was there, since we hadn't really been kicking it. Beans was making that shit hard as hell with her annoying ass. Every time I turned around, it was *the baby need this, the baby need that.* On top of that, because she'd been kicked out of her place, I allowed her and the baby to stay at my crib until next month. That's when the apartment I'd rented out would be available for her to move in. Having her at my place had definitely put a pause on me and Yaz's relationship. Even though she was still cordial with me, her actions showed me that she wasn't with the shits. Honestly, I couldn't blame her. I really thought I'd be over the moon in love with my son, but I couldn't really enjoy the moment from the drama that was attached to him. Shit was aggy as fuck.

I grabbed the duffle bag full of dope and got out of my car. Making my way up to the front door, I knocked lightly.

"Come in!" Nova called out, as I entered the house. The first face I saw was Yaz's as she sat on the sectional in the front room. Nova was sitting across from her, but I wasn't paying her no attention. I only had eyes for one lady, and I was sure she knew who it was. "Wassup

Smoke?"

"Same ole thang," I responded. "Yaz, what's good?" I asked, trying to break the ice.

"Everything is good over my way," she responded with a nonchalant smile. "How's the baby?"

"He's good and getting fatter by the day."

"He's about two months old now, right?" Nova asked.

"Yea, two and a half months to be exact," I answered.

"Cool. I've yet to see him in person," Nova said.

"That's because his dumb ass ugly mama be tripping. She don't want her child around me or nobody else but Smoke. She don't even let him go around his mama too funny."

"Damn, you got a baby mama like that?" Nova pondered with a shake of the head, but I could tell that Yaz had already filled her in.

"Hell yea, and the shit is working my nerves. I'll just be glad when she can move into her apartment before she drive me crazy," I said.

"I bet," Nova chimed in.

"Anyway, she's the last thing I wanna discuss. Where is Tam at?"

"She left with Heavy not long ago," Nova answered.

"Ok, well, I'll talk with y'all and she can be filled in later."

"Ok," Nova said, as Yaz just sat waiting to hear

what I had to say. "Sit down then."

"In the past two and half months since y'all have been working, the drops have been off some weeks and on point other weeks."

"I know and I hope that y'all know we don't have nothing to do with that," Nova quickly said.

"We know and we believe we know who's behind it," I said.

"It's Monk," Yaz chimed in. "I've always had a feeling that he was shady and this proves it."

"We definitely believe it's Monk too," I said.

"He's a real asshole," Yaz told me. "I try not to tell Rah everything because I know how he is, but maybe it's time for him to get dealt with."

"Say less," Smoke assured me in so little words. "I know y'all feel safer with your guns on you but, for the next couple of drops, me, Heavy or Jose will be chaperoning y'all."

"Dang, we ain't had a chaperone since we've been strapped," Yaz said.

"I know, but we feel it's best. Plus, we'd rather y'all be safe than sorry," I told them.

"If that's how y'all really feel, then we have no choice but to roll with that," Nova said, but I could tell she had gotten used to running shit on her own with only her girls on her side. It gave her power and power was a dangerous thing if she didn't play her cards right. Either way, we'd have their backs.

"So, this has nothing to do with Rah or the business, but have you heard from Kobe lately?"

"He hit me up a couple of times since he's been gone. Both times I was too busy to talk with him and didn't answer. He'd text and ask that I call him back, but I never do."

"I wouldn't mind talking to him myself, but I don't want to overstep my boundaries. Maybe I should just leave well enough alone. It would be interesting to talk to someone that resembles Kirk. I think I wanna see what the good version of Kirk looks like. Just to hear that he's a doctor says a lot about his character. I always said that Kirk was smart as hell, he just never applied himself to the fullest."

"I can totally agree with that," Nova said. "I believe that's why I've been dodging him though. It's just a strange feeling being in his presence."

"I can imagine," I responded. Just thinking about it made me feel funny inside. I was sure it would be strange as hell sitting in a room talking to a Kirk look-a-like.

"It's interesting how Mrs. Koban allowed that to happen. Regardless of what she was going through, I could never see her giving up her child. But, then again, that would explain how absent she was in Kirk's life. Hell, it probably bothered her to be around him knowing that his twin wasn't there."

Nova agreed with me. "I definitely thought about this over and over again, and those are my same thoughts. I'm sure it was very hard for her. I think that Mr. Koban could've done something about it, but he allowed the shit to play out the way he did. Maybe he didn't want that doctor guy around. After all, she'd already been cheating with him. I think it was easier to just let him take his son while they took Kirk and to close that book completely."

"Yea, but then he's the one that calls and tells him the minute he finds out about Kirk," Yaz chimed in.

"Maybe he'd been feeling guilty all these years and, after hearing that news, it probably hit him," Nova said.

"Sounds about right." I nodded. "Well, if he calls back, tell him to call me. That way you won't have to deal with him no more."

"And you do?" she asked.

"I'm just curious about him. I can't lie about that."

"Okaaaaay," Nova responded.

"Well, Rah told me that he wanted to leave this here," I said, looking at the duffle bag filled with product. "He's sliding through in the morning to pick it up. You know he's always pushing for time, and it'll be easier to come here and then make his rounds than to go all the way back to the country and then back to town."

"I know. He prides himself on being punctual." Nova nodded with a smile.

"You're definitely getting to know him," I teased.

"I can't wait till he gets back. I miss him."

"Girl, he's only been gone two days," Yaz clowned.

"Two days too long," Nova teased back.

I simply laughed. They always had a way of picking at each other.

"Well, I'll take this off your hands," Nova said as she picked up the duffle bag. "This thing is heavy. I'm gonna tell Rah when I talk to him that I know he only wants to come here first because he's missing me like crazy too."

"I'm sure that also has a lot to do with it," I concurred. Once she was out of sight, I looked over at Yaz. "I've missed you."

She slightly smiled. "I've missed you too."

"So, let me come over to see you later."

Slightly, she shook her head. "You know I want to, but I'm not fooling around as long as Beans is under your roof. I think she plays dirty and I don't want no parts of that. I been done beat her ass, I ain't gon' lie."

"She is asking for it," I uttered. "I can't apologize enough about this situation. I know it's hard for you. Hell, it's hard for me. Beans is not the woman that I've known all these years. It's like pregnancy changed her. This baby has changed her. Somehow, she thinks that we're supposed to be together, but that ain't happening. I've had that talk with her several times. I think it only makes her colder. She even said once that we should get married."

"What?! I know damn well she ain't talking like that."

"Shit, I was shocked as hell when she said it too."

"She acts like she's trying to lock you in, but she's doing it by any means necessary."

"And that shit don't work for me."

"So, does the baby have any of your features yet?"

"He's just a baby, so it's hard to tell. Mama keeps saying to do a paternity test and I mentioned it to Beans.

195

However, that pissed her all the way off."

Yaz frowned. "She shouldn't get that bothered by it if he is yours."

"I just don't see why she would lie about something like that."

"I think she'd lie because she knows that you'll take care of her and the baby. She knows you won't let them down. But another man, on the other hand, just might. What do you know about Beans when it comes to other men? Did y'all ever share those conversations?"

"Well, I did all the time, but she was a little more secretive about her shit."

"So, do you see where I'm coming from?" Yaz pondered.

I couldn't help but nod my head. "I do. Don't think I've not thought about this because I have. So, I've gotten one of those home tests and I plan on using it the minute Beans isn't around. For her sake, I hope it comes back that he's mine because if not, this will destroy our friendship and anything that's attached to it."

"For her sake, I hope so too. But, for my sake, I hope not because I might have to walk away from this relationship. I'm not going to allow that type of energy in my space. One thing I know is that she'll always make trouble for us."

I disappointedly shook my head. It was nothing I could say to that because she was right. So, I got up to leave. Hugging her tightly and kissing her softly on the forehead, I gazed in her eyes and said, "I'm not leaving you. I don't care what you say or how you feel. I love you and, if this baby is mine, Beans ain't gon' have a choice but to accept that. Son or no son, she gotta know that. She won't control me because of him. Either she'll come around, or she'll lose me being in his life. I can always take care of him without dealing with her crazy ass."

Yaz smiled and, to my surprise, she grabbed my face to kiss my lips. I hadn't had a kiss like that in forever. It definitely felt good, but I wasn't going to press my luck. I could tell that she knew where my heart was and that's all I needed from her. I was determined to get that blood test done, so I could move forward in whatever steps I had to take. I wasn't losing my woman for nobody, that was for sure.

17

Nova Thang

I rolled over and opened my eyes to see this handsome man standing over me. A big smile appeared on my face, as he smiled back at me. He was indeed what many women called a pretty boy and, not to mention, fine as fuck.

"Good morning Hermosa."

"Good morning Handsome," I said while clearing the old lady out of my throat.

"Tam let me in, I hope you don't mind."

"I never mind you coming in here," I responded. Hell, he could have a key too, but I wasn't going to move that fast so soon. Plus, I didn't want him to know that I was ridin' his dick this hard. "You know I love when you visit."

Rah smiled. "Get up and put some clothes on. I'm gonna take you out to breakfast before I get my day started."

"Awww, how sweet." I smiled. "You sure you don't want to crawl in bed with me first?"

"Don't tempt me, but I need to stay focused on the day and what I have on my agenda."

I figured he would say that, or he would've already been in the bed with me. Rah was like no other. Business seemed to always come first. Whatever he had planned for the day would most likely go just as he'd planned. He never went off course. I think it was something that they all pride themselves on and why business always ran so smoothly and stayed on track.

"Okaaaaay," I playfully pouted as I slid out of bed. The minute my feet hit the floor, Rah pulled me close to him and softly kissed my lips. I don't believe that there was feeling that was better than that. I smiled, not wanting him to let me go, but I knew he was eager to get his day started. I was just glad that he was making time to spend some of it with me. "Give me a second. I just need to freshen up right quick," I told him.

"Where's that bag at?"

"It's in the closet," I told him, as I headed into the bathroom. A few minutes later, I returned to join him, as he looked through the duffle bag.

"Is everything good?"

"Yea, everything's here. I just wished I would've gotten Smoke to get a few more. I'm going to test Monk this week. I need to know what he really got going on."

"Monk's a real asshole," I uttered.

"Do I need to replace him?" he asked, giving me a serious stare.

"Nah, I can handle myself."

"It's not about you handling yourself. I just don't want you dealing with someone that's not fully respecting your position."

I really wanted to say more, but I could handle myself. Plus, I didn't want Rah to see me as being weak if I continued to speak on Monk's unpredictable behavior. "Look, I'm good. He respects us for what it's worth. He knows not to cross that line. On top of that, we all walk in there strapped now. They don't know we carry guns, but we'll use 'em if we have to."

Rah smiled. "Look at my lil thug in the making. Would you really use that gun if you had to?"

"Damn right, I would," I responded with a smirk.

"You'll never need to use it though. I just wanted y'all to carry them for safety. Just in case," he added. "However, niggas know not to fuck with you or your crew. They'd die behind that. Those are facts."

"I know," I said while thinking about Kirk's demise. I was sure he wished he would've done things differently or treated me kinder. "I thank you for always having my back," I said while slipping on my clothes.

"You don't ever have to thank me for that. Any real man gon' always make sure his lady good."

His lady? I pondered to myself. He had never referred to me as his lady. I smiled inside, feeling giddy as hell. But, I didn't want to speak on it, just in case he didn't realize what he had said.

"You ready?"

"Yes," I said, after putting my hair in a ponytail. "Let's go."

"Okay, I'm gonna put this bag in the closet, so I'm not unnecessarily riding around with it."

"That's cool," I told him. Once he put the bag up, he and I headed out for the morning. I didn't even bother telling Tam because I was sure she was still knocked out after the drunken night we'd had full of laughs and good conversation.

****

We pulled up to a breakfast spot called *That Flippin' Egg*. This was the second time that Rah had brought me here. That was one thing about him. He always paid attention to the things I said, and once I mentioned that I enjoyed their famous chicken and waffles. From that point on, anytime he had free time, which wasn't very often, he'd treat me out to eat for breakfast. This was normally our place to go. I wasn't crazy about nobody else's breakfast unless it was my parents doing the cooking.

I pulled down the visor to check my face right quick. I wanted to make sure that I was on point, which was something I always did before stepping out of a car. Then, I grabbed my purse, as Rah turned off the engine. He got out of the car and walked around to open the door for me. He was definitely a gentleman and I appreciated it. Kirk didn't open doors unless he knew I was pissed with him or unless he was in a decent mood. Dating Rah was a lot different in many ways.

"Let's go shawty," he teased, as I smiled. As we were walking up to the doors of the restaurant, Rah paused in his steps. Before I could even notice what was going on, a woman walked over to us. *Okaaaay*, I immediately thought. I mean, I knew Rah was a known person, so my instincts was to just peep game.

"Well, hey Raheem," the woman said with a

friendly smile.

"Wassup," Rah spoke back.

"I didn't expect to see you here."

"Likewise," Rah coolly responded.

"I meant to text you back last night, but I fell asleep. Thanks for helping me get moved in," she mentioned, as my eyes darted from her then back to Rah's expression.

"Well, I didn't do nothing but point you in the right direction. Nothing more or less," he nonchalantly told her.

"And I appreciated that," she said and looked over at me. "As long as I've known you, I never really saw you out with nobody. Not in this manner," she teased with a slight smirk on her face.

"And what manner is that?" I pondered, now clearly invading on their conversation.

"Oh, Rah doesn't take women out on dates unless he's really feeling them. Trust me, it hasn't been too many of us in his life," she responded. "Nevertheless, I'm not going to hold y'all. It was good seeing you, Raheem."

"Have a good one," Rah said and grabbed me gently by the hand. "Let's go in." We walked off, but I could tell that the woman wanted to entertain me a little longer with her shenanigans, but Rah wasn't with it.

The minute we sat down, I grabbed my menu and pretended to be looking through it. I'm sure this was unusual because I always ate the same thing. I didn't need a menu at all. Not being able to hold off any longer, I simply dropped the menu on the table, looked him in the eyes and asked. "Who was that woman?"

"An old friend," he responded.

"She sounded more than just an old friend," I said, shooting him a playful side-eye. I didn't want to seem too serious. I just wanted the truth.

"She's someone I had dealings with in the past."

"Was it just in the past? You did say that you pointed her in the right direction."

"Yea, I did. She hit me up because she was moving back to the city. She wanted to know if I knew of a moving company that she could use at a discounted rate and I simply pointed her in the right direction. No more or less," Rah explained. "But we'll talk more about this if you must when I return," he said, getting up from the table. "I'm heading to the restroom."

"Okay," I said, just as the waitress walked over.

"What will you be having to drink?" she asked me.

"Can I get two glasses of orange juice, two glasses of water, and two breakfast plates of your chicken and waffles with strawberry butter?"

"Yes ma'am. I'll be right back with your drinks."

"Thank you," I responded. Once she walked off, I started going through my cell phone, just being nosy on social media. However, my thoughts were still on the woman that approached us. She was a beautiful lady with straight white teeth and a ponytail pulled up that was longer than mine. Just from her early morning attire, I could tell she was a bit bougie wearing a white Chanel romper with the Saint Laurent white heels. She carried a Chanel purse with the matching Chanel bracelet, watch and necklace. She seemed like Rah's type but, then again, not really. I guess it just depended on his taste at the moment. Maybe she was just there for a reason and a season because I knew he wanted someone that was down to ride for the long haul. Not just a pretty face with a nice body.

"Uh, excuse me," the light voice said, as I looked up from my cell phone.

"Oh, it's you again."

"Yes, it's me again." She smiled. "My name is Ginger and I'm Raheem's ex-girlfriend."

"Okaaaaay," I responded, like what's your point shawty?

"I just had to circle back, not wanting to start nothing with you. You seem like a really sweet person. I just know that Raheem isn't ready for a new relationship. I can tell by the things we talk about."

"How often do y'all talk?" I pondered.

"We talk a lot, especially since I've been back here. I just don't want you getting your hopes up high and then be let down. I intend on getting back with him."

"I'd prefer if Rah told me this. Otherwise, I think this conversation is irrelevant. It's not really nothing you can say to make me feel any differently."

"Okay, well, don't say I didn't warn you," she smirked. I could slap that smug expression right off her face, but I was going to let her have that. "If you think I'm lying, check his cell phone. I mean, look at his messages between us. His phone's code is his deceased uncle's full birthday. I'm almost positive he hasn't changed it," she said. "Anyway, it was nice to meet you."

She walked off, leaving me sitting there not knowing whether to be pissed off or not. I felt like she had tried me on the low and I didn't like that. However, I quickly straightened my face up when Rah joined me at the table.

"You good?" he asked the minute he sat down. From the looks of things, he didn't know that I'd been approached by his ex and, for now, I was going to leave it at that.

"Yea, I'm good. I ordered for you."

"Preciate that love," he said while reaching across the table and gently caressing the back of my hand. "So, what more did you need to know from our earlier conversation?"

"Uh, nothing more. Let's just eat and enjoy our morning," I responded.

****

The ride back to my crib was somewhat quiet. I was trying not to be so obvious in my feelings, but home-girl had gotten a little under my skin. She was smug, irritating, and annoying as fuck with her predictions about my relationship, or lack thereof; let her tell it. I felt like me and Rah were in a good space. However, she apparently knew something that I didn't know.

Once back at the crib, Rah and I headed straight inside to find Tam in the kitchen cooking pancakes.

"Wassup lovebirds," she teased.

Rah grinned. "Wassup?"

"Hey girl. I see your butt was hungry," I said, as Rah headed straight down the hall to my bedroom.

"Yea, I was. I woke up with a slight headache, so that I meant I needed to put something on my stomach. Where y'all been?"

"Out to eat breakfast," I responded, just as Rah called out to me.

"Sounds like somebody wants more than just breakfast," Tam teased.

"Hush girl," I said with a big smile on my face. I didn't realize he wanted some ass but, hell, I was just as eager as he was. The minute I entered the bedroom, the look on his face was that of confusion. "What's wrong?"

"Where's the duffle bag?" he asked.

"Huh?" I asked, walking over to the closet. "The duffle bag was in here. You saw it there before we left."

"I know, but where's it at now?"

Immediately, my heart dropped. *WHAT THE FUCK?!* I quickly thought to myself. I hurried out of the bedroom and down the hall. I didn't stop until I was face to face with Tam. "Who been here this morning?"

"CJ left right before y'all got here. He was here talking and joking around and, the next minute, he was gone."

"What you mean, GONE?"

"I mean, I told him I was going in the bathroom to freshen up and, by the time I came out, he was gone. But

I bet you I took my purse in there with me. That nigga wasn't gonna get me again," she joked with laughter.

"He may not have gotten you—"

"That's because he got me," Rah instantly cut in.

I didn't even realize he was standing there, as my mouth dropped wide open. This shit had to be unreal. CJ had surely barked up the wrong tree and not even I could help him down from this one.

18

Tamara "Tam" Newton

"So, you say this pussy ass nigga stole money from you too?" Heavy asked. I knew the nigga was heated, but I didn't want to make the situation worse.

"Well, yea, but he later paid me back," I hesitantly responded.

"I'm just pissed the fuck off that I'm finding out about this shit. It's been two fucking weeks, and nobody heard from him? I bet I could've located his ass," Heavy fussed. "I know my cousin trying to take it easy on this nigga because that's Nova's brother, but I would've had his head by now."

Which is why he waited to tell you, I thought to myself. "Rah had been waiting to see if he would contact Nova or their parents, so he could talk with him. CJ is somewhat a complicated person. I can't really explain it, but if you know, you know," I said, but Heavy wasn't trying to hear it.

"The nigga got sticky fingers, but he done messed with the wrong man's shit."

"Babe, calm down."

"Nawl, I'm blowed about this shit. I can't believe you didn't tell me."

"I didn't tell you because Rah asked me not to. He knows you would've blown a fuse and he didn't want that to happen. So, I just wanted to respect what he had asked of me and waited for him to tell you, instead."

"This shit is unbelievable. That was over one-hundred thousand dollars of work. Did you know that?"

My eyes widened, but I tried to hold my composure. "I didn't know the exact amount, but I was sure that it was a lot."

"Damn right it was a lot," Heavy bickered with an angry shake of the head.

At that time, Rah entered back in the house. He walked straight over to Heavy. I stood back, not wanting to be a part of this shit. It was just too much tension in the air.

"Cuz, you need to chill out. I can hear you all the way outside and you know Nova just pulled up on the estate."

"I can't help it. I feel like this lil pussy ass nigga done tried us. Does he even know who he's fucking with?!"

"Apparently not, and that's why I'm trying to give him a chance to talk to me. I don't want to hurt him, but I will if he don't comply."

"Well, he's asking for it. It's been two fucking weeks. If he ain't called by now, then it's only right that we teach his ass a lesson."

"I don't' wanna do that Cuz," Rah said. "Not yet." I could tell he was stuck between pussy and hard place. Pussy had his ass on lock and key, but he really wanted to knock CJ's block off, literally.

"Something's gotta be done. Our people are gonna be asking questions soon."

"And that's why I told you. We gotta make up something, so they don't trip too hard. This shit happened on my watch. I'm responsible for it. I just can't go out bad like that."

"Which is why he gotta be dealt with. You know if we deal with it, then it lessens the blow when they find out that we're missing that much product."

"Don't you know I know that," Rah said. "But you gotta chill out. Don't go doing nothing just yet. I need him alive."

"Well, the nigga better hurry up and talk or he's a dead man walking," Heavy said, just as Nova entered the house with an alarmed expression look on her face.

"I hope I wasn't interrupting nothing serious," she said.

"No, no," Rah answered as he rushed over to her. "You're good. Me and Heavy was just talking. Look, chill out for a minute with Tam. I'm gonna step outside and talk with Heavy, then we'll leave when I'm done," he said.

"Okay," Nova said. The minute they were out of sight, she looked over at me. "They're gonna kill him, aren't they?"

"Nooooo, don't say that. Rah doesn't want to do anything to him. You know this or he would've been gotten dealt with."

"Yea, but he can only control Heavy for so long."

"That's true, but Heavy is not going to do nothing of that caliber without Rah's permission. You also know that. He's just mad because he didn't know."

"For good reason," Nova uttered. "I'm so mad with CJ. His ass won't return none of our calls. He's running around like a mad man still taking people's shit and I'm sick of it. I thought he had gotten his shit together when he paid you your money back. But, let's be real, he more than likely stole from Paul just to pay Peter."

"This time he done stole from God, and now his ass has run into a brick wall with nowhere to go—"

"And soon it'll be nowhere to hide," Nova chimed in. "I just don't know what to say."

"Well, don't think too hard about it. Hopefully, he comes around."

"Yea but, if he do, the question is will he have all that work he took?"

I simply shook my head. "I doubt it," I responded.

"I don't wanna talk about this no more. How are you and Heavy?" Nova asked, clearly trying to change the subject.

"Things are great. Well, except for now. His daughter is upstairs sleeping; she stayed here with us last night."

"Aww, that's sweet." Nova smiled. "She's a pretty little thing."

"Isn't she?" I agreed. "I'm growing to love her. Hell, I'm starting to love all of his kids. Me and the baby mamas get along fine. It's just that other one." I shook my head.

"Talking about her mother?" Nova asked, glancing upstairs.

"Yea, her mammy," I joked. "She is such a bitch when she wants to be. Sometimes, I don't even know where I stand because Heavy doesn't really straighten her like he should. Maybe that's because I'm really not his woman. Not the way I feel like I should be."

"Don't say that. The nigga loves you."

"Well, I'm glad you see it. I won't believe that unless he says it or unless he straightens her ass. I'm already feeling like her time is running out with me. The bitch better count her days. She ain't got but one more time and I'm gon' put these hands on her."

Nova chuckled. "Lawd, I needed that laugh," she said as her eyes deflected over on the countertop. "Is that Rah's cell phone?"

"Yea, why?" I asked, giving her the side-eye.

"Well—"

"Don't you do it. Don't follow up that bitch. She just want yo' man back, but don't give her that satisfaction."

"Fuck that, it keeps staying on my mind, so I wanna know if he's been talking to her."

"Oh LAWD," I sighed, as she picked up his cell phone. "I'm peeking out the window, so your crazy ass don't get caught."

"So, his uncle's birthday is 03.14.59," she said, punching in the numbers.

"How you find that out?"

"It's written on a calendar that's on his refrigerator."

"Did it work?" I asked, glancing back over my shoulder and back out the window.

"Yep," she said, now scrolling through his phone.

"Girrrrrrl, you are violating to the fullest."

"I know, so hush. Just look out for me."

"I got you, bitch. They out in the yard still talking."

"Okay, good," she said.

"So, what did you find?" I nosily pondered.

"Ummm, oh, here she is," Nova said with eager eyes. "He has the bitch saved under *My EX*. And EX is in capital letters girl."

I laughed. "Don't sound like he's trying to get back with her to me."

"Well, they've been talking but he's pretty much short talking her ass," Nova said, and then got quiet. "This message is a couple of months ago and she's talking about she enjoyed him last night."

"Whet?! Stop lying!"

"I'm serious," Nova said.

"They coming back girl!" I said, hurrying away from the window. Nova quickly put the phone back on the counter. "Anyway, what is Yaz doing?" I asked, trying to change the subject before the fellas walked back in the house.

"She and Smoke was at her house the last I talked to her. They have a lot going on."

"Who has a lot going on?" Heavy asked as he entered the house first, with Rah right behind him.

"Yaz and Smoke," I answered. "With your nosey butt."

Heavy laughed. "Yea, yea," he responded.

"You ready lil lady?" Rah asked.

"Yes, I'm ready," Nova responded, but I could tell that the only thing she was ready for was cussing his ass out. I just hoped she didn't fly off too fast without knowing all the facts first.

"Grab my phone," Rah told her. They said their *see you laters* and were on their way.

I glanced over at Heavy. "You don't think he's cheating on her, do you?"

Heavy frowned. "Now, where the hell did that come from?"

"I was just asking. You know how Nova is. She gets so wired up sometimes."

"She thinks too much. My cousin ain't cheating on her. Hell, this the first time he ain't been interested in another woman since they've been talking. I don't know what she did to him, but he's definitely all in."

"Okay, good," I said with a smile. Hearing that made me feel better. "Come here, give me some sugar. Maybe we can get it in right quick." I seductively grinned.

"Damn, that sounds good, but baby mama just got

here to pick up my snicker-doodle."

"Oh yea, I didn't see her."

"Huh?"

"Oh nothing," I responded, almost telling on myself. "Well, we can get to that once they leave."

"Sounds like a plan I'm down for," Heavy said, just as Simone barged through the door. "Damn, what happened to knocking first or ringing the doorbell?"

"Why would I do that when you already knew I was here? Didn't the security guard at the gate call you?"

"Yea but—"

"But nothing," Simone irritably said. "I didn't know you had company."

Heavy frowned. "It wasn't your business," he responded.

"What did I tell you about having this bitch around my daughter? Was she here with her all night too?"

"Yea—"

"And," I cut in, as I eased closer to her.

"And I don't want you around my daughter, bitch! What part—"

BOW!

I had smacked that bitch so hard, she couldn't even finish her sentence. As I had my hand wrapped in her weave, I began to punch her ass in the face.

"Y'all cut this shit out!" Heavy yelled as he attempted to pull me off her. That hair was so tightly gripped in my hand that I snatched that bitch whole wig off.

"AAAAAAHHHHH!!" she screamed out, as he carried her outside and gave me that look to sit my ass down somewhere.

I sat down but, the minute that door shut, I was peeking right back out that window.

"You let that bitch jump on me while my daughter in the house?!"

"She's sleep, but you shouldn't have been talking about her like that. What you think? She just gonna keep taking that smart-ass mouth of yours? Hell, you lucky I pulled her off you."

"Go get my child and she's not allowed over here no more while you're talking to her!"

"Fine, keep her away from me if that's what you wanna do. But, I'm gonna be with Tam whether you like it or not. That's my lady now and, no, I won't be fucking around with you no more. I'll make sure my daughter is good from afar. Hopefully, one day you'll come to your senses but, until you do, I'm okay with that."

My eyes widened from the shock of him actually telling her that. I wanted to cry because I was so happy. But I hurried back to the couch to sit down, as Heavy made his way in the house.

"You a'ight?" he asked.

"Yea, I'm okay," I said.

"We'll talk about this when I get back."

He headed up the stairs, as I continued to smile in

the inside. I knew without a doubt that I was going to fuck his brains out and I might even do it with this bitch six-hundred-dollar wig on.

19

Yazmine "Yaz" Gates

I rested my head on my man's chest feeling rather good that we had been getting things back on track. He was definitely the love of my life and it was no other man that could take his place. We still had the blood test results looming over our heads, but I didn't want that to deter what we were sharing at the moment.

"How you feeling?" I pondered.

"I feel pretty good, especially laying here with you."

I smiled because I felt the same way. "How has things been with your mom since you found out who your real family is?"

"She still won't talk about it," he answered. "So, I'm not pushing the issue no more. As long as I know, that's all that matters."

"I feel you."

"Rah and the family have welcomed me with open arms. It's nice being a part of the clan. They have so much going on, but I love how close they are. I really wish that my real father was here. Maybe I would've known love like that at the start of my life. But, then again, I'm told that my father wasn't really like them. I mean, he was definitely a hustler, but he was also a man of his own. He was the loner out of the bunch. He always stayed away from home, roaming the country and enjoying life. Being obedient to the family wasn't in his cards. That's probably why he's not with us today. He was hard-headed and wouldn't listen to nobody. I think besides the undeniable features, we really didn't have none of that other stuff in common. I'm very family oriented and I have no problems listening to advice or doing as I'm told, if I know it's for the best."

"Yea, I can agree with that."

"My mom is just stubborn, and I think she's been over it a long time ago. That's one reason why she doesn't care to relive it or talk about it. She ain't with the shits. Yea, she hates that I was raised by a woman beater, with his scary ass. I'm sure she regrets dealing with him, but she doesn't regret moving on from my real father and trying to have a life without him. I was told that he wasn't the type to hit women, but he definitely put my mom through a stressful time. The cheating was unbearable for her because she had so much love for him. Although I'm told that he loved her too, he just couldn't sit still long enough to settle. Even when he'd gotten married, he still ran the streets. So, I just think there probably wouldn't have ever been someone for him. Unfortunately, it was the pussy that ultimately killed him. Isn't that crazy because pussy was something he had control over for so long. It's crazy, I know."

"That is crazy," I uttered.

"I know we're on a good page here and I'm not trying to change that, but what if these results come back and the baby is mine?"

"I think that Beans is going to try to make it hard for us to be together. I also think I'll end up beating her ass."

Smoke laughed out loud. "I can see that."

"I'm so for real."

"I know."

"Anyway, I don't want to let her win because if I fall back, that's exactly what she wants. Truth is that I love you and I don't want to lose you. We'll just have to figure out a way of dealing with her and you still being able to be with your son."

"My son?" he said, like he was questioning it. "He just doesn't seem like he's mine. I don't know. It's weird but I don't have that attraction with him and, if he is mine, it'll only make me feel worse. I already feel like I'm letting him down and I don't want to be like my father or the man that raised me. I'm better than that and it hurts that I can't be there for him until I know the truth."

"When are the results supposed to come back?"

"Anytime now," he answered. "I'm so anxious, I don't know what to do with myself. This has really bothered me since I did it. Beans don't even know that I did it."

"Well, if he's yours, you won't have to say nothing about it."

"But, if he's not, all hell is gonna break loose. It's simply hard to fathom that she'd lie all this time, and for what?"

"If it's a lie, she had her reasons. I've already spoke

on that but, for her sake, she better hope she ain't lying."

"Me and Beans have always been better than that though. So, for her to just pop up out the blue with this news is something that I just can't see her doing, especially if it's a lie. The only reason why I wanted to get that test is because I don't see myself in that kid. He's just a baby, but I don't believe he's even mixed. Don't get me wrong, he has beautiful hair, he's beautiful himself, but I don't see the bloodline there."

"Well, we'll just have to—" I said, just as his cell phone buzzed of an incoming message. Eagerly, he picked it up, which caused me to pause mid-sentence. "Who is that?" I nosily pondered.

Smoke looked in his phone with anxious eyes. "It's the test results."

My eyes widened. "Wow, we talked that shit up."

"We did," he agreed.

"What does it say?"

"I don't know. I haven't even opened it to see yet."

"Why you nervous?"

"Just a lil bit and I don't even know why. I got the test for a reason."

"Well, read it," I urged him. Hell, I was more anxious than he was. I wanted to know too.

As silence set in, I sat as still as a statue trying to hold my composure. Hell, it felt like I was even holding my breath. *Breathe bitch breathe,* I coached myself. I didn't know what the damn results said but, if I could snatch his phone and see it for myself, I would've.

Smoke looked over at me with an expression that was hard to read. I didn't know if he was happy, disappointed, or what. It was the blankest look I had ever seen.

"Get dressed. We're heading to my crib."

"Huh? What did the test say?"

"Just get dressed. I have some apologizing to do and it can't be done unless it's in front of the both of you."

I got out of bed. I didn't know what the fuck was going on, but Smoke was straight tripping. If the baby was his, all he had to do was say it. I didn't need no damn surprises, that was for sure. However, I wanted closure when it came to this situation, so I would go. I just hoped that it would be worth it.

****

The ride over to Smoke's crib was quiet as fuck. By the time we made it there, I was sitting on pens and needles. I couldn't believe this nigga hadn't disclosed the information of that paternity test yet. He had to know that I was driving myself crazy wondering what the hell was going on. Once we parked, he wasted no time getting out the car, and I didn't either. I was hot on his heels as we headed straight to the front door and walked inside.

"I was wondering if you were going to come back home. Me and the baby thought you had run away." Beans grinned, as she held the little one while watching TV. She hadn't even looked back to notice that Smoke wasn't by himself. So, when he went and stood in front of the TV blocking her view, she finally saw me standing there too. "Oh hey, Yazmine. I didn't know you were with him," she dryly said.

"Hey Beans," I dryly spoke back. It was obvious she didn't know what the hell was going on, neither did I, but we were both about to find out.

"Move from in front of the TV. I'm trying to look at POWER."

"I think POWER can wait," Smoke said in a serious tone.

"What now?" Beans asked. "Every time you hang around your lil girlfriend, you come back home with an attitude," she spat.

"His lil girlfriend?" I pondered, wishing I could slap the taste out of her mouth.

"Yea, his lil girlfriend because you're not his son's mother. So, what am I supposed to call you?"

"Nawl, we ain't doing this today. Both of y'all be quiet," Smoke insisted. I wanted to retaliate but I would let them have that. "Speaking of my son. I had a DNA test taken—"

"You had a what?" Beans cut in while standing to her feet with the baby in her arms. "I know damn well you ain't took a test of my baby with me not knowing about it."

"I did," Smoke responded. "I swabbed him with a home DNA kit test, and I swabbed myself. I sent it off about two weeks ago and the results are in."

"Okay, and he's yours. So, what's the issue?"

"The issue is that he's not mine and I believe you knew it."

Beans' eyes widened like she was on an episode of

Maury. If she could've hauled ass backstage and fell out crying, she would've. "Stop lying. Let me see the results."

"I don't have to let see nothing. You already know the truth. Now, if you want us to take this to an actual facility and have the test done again, I'm ready. I can't believe that you've been lying all this time and for what, Beans?"

Beans stood there in silence with her mouth dropped open. Sister girl acted like the cat had her tongue.

Shit, I was in shock too as I looked over at Smoke and asked. "Can I see?" Hell, I wanted to see the shit myself.

Smoke wasted no time handing me his phone, so I could see the results and, true enough, it was 0% probability that he was the father. I looked at Beans, wanting to shake my head but I didn't. I knew this had to be an embarrassing moment for her.

"Smoke, why wouldn't you talk to me about this instead of involving her?" Beans asked.

"Because you've been a real bitch to her, and you've been using the fuck outta me. Why Beans? We were once tight as thieves. We were best friends. You didn't have to lie to me! I would've still been there for you and the baby. Hell, I would've even been the God father had you asked me, but why would lie about that baby being mine?"

"I don't want to talk about this right now, especially in front of her. I'll get our shit and leave," she said like she was hurting somebody.

"Where will you go? Your apartment won't be ready until next month?"

"I'll find someplace for us to go. I don't need this disrespect from you or her."

I frowned. "I haven't even said nothing disrespectful, so I don't know why you feel that way."

"Don't talk to me," she said with a roll of the eyes.

"She don't have to talk to you and neither do I. But I'm not a heartless guy. I won't put you out just because I do feel sorry for your baby."

"We don't need your pity."

"I never said you did, but you apparently needed something because you're here."

At that time, Beans just started crying. I had no sympathy for the hoe, but Smoke did. Bless his heart.

"Beans, whatever you're going through is not the end of the world. You have a baby now you have to think about him. I don't know what your reason was for telling me that he was mine, but I don't even want to go there. I just know that he's not and I'm not going to play this little game with you anymore. I don't mind you staying here until your apartment is ready. I will still pay the bills there for at least six months, hopefully you'll get it together. But, this ain't it Beans. You nearly destroyed my relationship. Do you know that?"

Beans just kept crying and shaking the baby at the same time. I was sure his lil cute butt was wondering what the hell was going on and if I could tell him, I'd say. *"Your dumb ass mama has really fucked up this time."* But since it wasn't my place, I'd keep that lil bit to myself.

"I really wanted to apologize to you, babe, because I wanted to believe her. I should've gotten solid evidence before I put our relationship on the line. She treated you bad and I'm sorry for that. Had I known early on, none of that would've happened. I love you and I want you to know that we're in this forever and you ain't gotta worry about another baby unless it's by you."

I was trying not to tear up, but the way this nigga looked at me showed his sincerity. I appreciated the way he stood up to Beans and apologized to me in front of her.

"Thank you, Baby. I love you too," I said back.

"Beans, you have nothing to say to her?" Smoke asked, now turning his attention back to her.

"No and again, I'll leave. I don't want to intrude on this bullshit. Thanks for nothing," she said with sarcasm and wasted no time leaving the room.

Smoke looked over at me with an unbothered shrug of the shoulders. I guess in his mind he didn't care no more. Beans was a grown ass woman. Either she'd take his act of kindness, even though she didn't deserve it, or she could leave. It was entirely up to her. All I knew was that me and my man was back on the best of terms and wasn't nan nother bitch going to come between us. That was for sure.

20

Nova Thang

I slept in late, as I was feeling extremely tired from all the bullshit that seemed to circle me. Rah had dropped me off around midnight after spending a little time with me, but I wasn't even in the mood for his company after going through his cell phone. I couldn't believe he had fucked that bitch and had been talking to her but acted like he hadn't. I mean, it wasn't many text messages from him but still he entertained the hoe. I didn't know if he had just fucked her to see if he still had feelings and then decided he didn't. But that text message she left him was quite revealing. If he was over her, that would explain why his messages seemed like he was just short talking her. Even I could see that, but the problem was that she didn't get the picture.

On top of that, Rah had informed me that we weren't going to make any more runs. He felt like Monk wasn't someone he could trust, and, because of that, he was pulling us out of the game, completely. I was somewhat heated because he'd just sprung that news on me, but I respected why. I couldn't lie, the money was damn good and, if anybody knew me, they knew I loved me some money. I could take more than a few vacations if I wanted to, but I had decided to get back in school.

As I laid there, my cell phone began to ring. I glanced down at the screen to see that it was Kobe calling me. With a frown on my face, I sent the call the voicemail. He never called me, so I was confused. But, just as I expected, he sent me a text message.

I know this is weird for you and I can understand why. I'm just still struggling with a lot of things that I'm unclear on. I'll be visiting the woman that gave me away later today and just wanted to know if you could find the time to meet with me. KOBE

A part of me felt bad as hell for him, but I just wasn't in the space of dealing with Kirk's brother. Not right now. However, I decided to call him back. On the first ring, he answered.

"Hey Nova," he answered like he'd known me forever.

"Hey Kobe, wassup? I just got your message."

"How are you?"

"I'm okay," I dryly responded.

"I don't want to be a pain, but I'm really just wanting to know more about my brother. It still bothers me that I'm just finding out about him, along with other things. I really just want some closure."

"I understand and, honestly, I think it's best if you speak with his best friend Smoke. He can probably fill you in on more things of interest when it comes to Kirk. See, your brother wasn't always bad when it came to me, but he wasn't always good either. He had a temper that would go from 0 to 100 real quick. He'd beat on me when he couldn't have his way, and he was a real shitty person to my parents. However, there were a lot of times when he'd spoil me, but that was only to make me stick around and overlook the abuse."

"Wow."

"Yea, wow is right," I commented. "So, I don't know what else I can tell you. I'm still shocked that Mrs. Koban has lived this lie for as long as she did, but I don't want no parts of it. I feel bad for you, but I'm just glad that it's another version of Kirk that's a good guy because clearly, he was dealing with demons of his own. On top of that, he didn't have many friends because of his unpredictable behavior. He was somewhat a loner, even though he had lots of money. The money came from him selling drugs for years," I revealed, just so he wouldn't ask. I didn't care how I spoke about Kirk. I wasn't going to sugar coat it and he could take it for what it was worth. I wasn't in the space of sitting down and talking with him because I wasn't comfortable with it and I wasn't going to pretend like I was.

Kobe had gotten quiet on the call. I didn't know what he expected me to say but, apparently, that wasn't it.

"You okay?" I pondered.

"Uh, yea," he responded.

"But, like I said, he has a best friend name Rashad. Well, we call him Smoke. He did tell me to tell you to call him and he'd talk with you about your brother. I hope that'll work for you because I'm done talking about him. I just want to move on with my life."

"I'm so sorry you had to deal with that. I don't

know why he was that way. I figured we had a lot in common, but maybe I was wrong. I would never treat my lady in such a way."

"Well, good for you," I said, sitting up in my bed. I hated giving him this shitty attitude, but I was dealing with a lot and him contacting me was just bad timing. However, I was tired of dodging him, so it was best to just got this overdue conversation over with.

"What are you doing in here? It's two in the afternoon and you're still in the bed," Tam teased as she barged in my bedroom.

I held up my finger to delay her loudmouth from continuing. "Hey Kobe, I hope I was of some help to you. Here is Smoke's number," I called the number out to him, hoping he was writing it down. "Please, call him if you would like to know more about your brother. Again, I'm sorry you're dealing with this and I hope that things work out for you."

"Thank you," Kobe responded.

"You're welcome, good-bye." Before he could say anything else, I ended the call.

"Daaaaaamn girl, that's how you feeling?" Tam expressed.

"Yes, girl. I'm so over that shit. I just needed him to know the real Kirk and I passed him on to Smoke. I don't wanna deal with that no more."

"Well, hell, I can't blame you. You went through a lot with that nigga, all the way up to the end."

"Exactly," I agreed.

"Anyway, I came in here to tell you that I beat Simone's ass last night."

"Stop lying!"

"I'm so serious. Long story short, the hoe tried me for the last time, and I put these hands on her ass."

"What the hell? What did Heavy do?"

"He broke it up, but it was too late. I had the bitch wig in my hand by the time it was over."

"Noooooo," I gasped.

"Yesssssss," Tam laughed. "I felt so relieved after that. Plus, Heavy took my side and told that bitch that he was going to be with me and that he wasn't fucking with her no more."

"For real?"

"Hell yea, guess I won that battle across the board."

"You did that. I'm happy for you."

"Thanks Sis. So, did you ask Rah about that shit in his phone?"

"Hell no. I ain't about to let him know that I went through his phone."

"Well, good because from what Heavy told me, that chick is delusional. She wants Rah back, but he ain't with it. She even sends him old messages in an attempt to jog his memory of how good they were together."

"What? Old messages? So, that message could've been an old one?"

"Yea, I'm almost 100% sure it was an old one."

"Wow, that bitch really had me going. It would explain why she was so desperate in approaching me at the restaurant—"

"And telling you to go through his phone."

"Riiiiight," I agreed. "Thank God I didn't confront him about that. He would've been pissed."

"More like livid," Tam expressed. "So, what do you think about them pulling us from picking up the drops?"

"Honestly, I'm only mad about missing out on the money, but I don't mind. I didn't expect that we'd be doing this forever. Hell, I only did it to prove a point to Rah that I could handle that lifestyle, but it's cool."

"Yea, you're right. Since Heavy has now said that he wants to be with me, I'm good either way. It was fun though, living like the Cartel for a few months."

"It was definitely something I never thought I would be doing. I'm taking my money and going back to school though. That's my calling."

"Aww, I'm happy for you."

"Thanks Sis," I said, just as my cell phone rang. I glanced down at the caller ID. "It's mama."

"You better answer that or she'll be on our doorstep," Tam joked.

"Hey Ma, what you doing?"

"Hey baby," she said, sounding like she was distressed and upset about something.

"What's wrong?"

"I need you to come to the hospital."

"Why, you okay? Where's daddy?" I asked, trying not to immediately panic.

"Daddy is right here. They found your brother earlier this morning."

"Who found him? Ma, who found him?" I asked again, since she'd gotten all quiet on the phone. All I could hear was sniffs from her side, and daddy's voice chimed in.

"Nova," he said, but I cut him off.

"Is he dead?!!"

"No baby, but he's been severely beaten and shot. He's in a coma right now. Just come to the hospital. If Tam or Yaz is there, get them to drive you," he said, followed by, "I love you. I'll see you soon."

"Love you too, dad." I said and ended the call. With tears in my eyes, I told Tam what was going on.

"I'll call Yaz. You get yourself together so we can go," Tam advised. I could tell she was just as distraught as I was, but she'd always been the strong one.

As I began to get dressed, thoughts began to run through my mind. Rand and I had already talked about this over and over again and he swore he wouldn't hurt my brother. However, Heavy was in on it now, so I didn't know what to think. All I know was if Rah was in on this, it would be a for sure deal breaker. I definitely couldn't be with a man that would put out a hit on my brother.

****

Two hours turned into four in no time, as I sat waiting on any kind of good news about my brother. Shit

233

was crazy. He was found in a back alley badly beaten and shot in his side. They had to remove a bullet during a two-hour surgery, and the strangest thing was that I'd called Rah but didn't get an answer. I didn't know what was going on with him, but his actions was telling me all I needed to know.

As I sat there by my mother, who was worried and upset, I didn't even know how to comfort her. CJ was my brother and I loved him dearly, but he was her child, so I could only imagine how awful she felt. My father was being strong, I could see the fear in his eyes. What if my brother didn't make it or wake up? That would be devastating for my family.

"Mom I'm going outside to join Yaz and Tam for some fresh air. Do you need anything?"

"No, sweetie."

"Dad?"

"No baby" he responded. "Go get some air. Better yet, you can even go home. There is nothing you can do here. I wish your mom would go with you."

"I'm not leaving my child for nothing or nobody,," Mama said in a serious tone.

"I know," Dad said.

"You sure, dad? I don't mind staying. I want to be here when CJ wakes up."

"Well, according to the doctors, no telling how long that'll be. But, I know better. He'll wake up soon, his body just needs to rest," Mama expressed. "So, go. Please, just go on home. I'll call you if anything changes."

I was somewhat hesitant but, clearly, I needed to leave because this shit was deep and I had to get to the bottom of things. "Love y'all," I said, hugging the both of them and leaving. Once outside, the looks on Tam and Yaz's faces were as if they were hiding something.

"Wassup with y'all?"

"Um, well, um, me and Yaz was talking and we're starting to think that maybe the fellas had something to do with this. I don't want to think they did but, when Heavy found out about your brother, he was determined to find him. I spoke with him about an hour ago and, at first, things seemed cool. He was talking to me like nothing happened. However, when I told him that we were at the hospital because of your brother, he got quiet. I asked him what was wrong and he told me that he'd call me back."

"Well, has he called you back?" I pondered.

"No, he hasn't. Not yet," she added.

"Fuck this, I'm riding out there," I said, now feeling some type of way. "If Rah had this done to my brother, I need to hear it from him."

"And what if he did, then what?"

"Then, I have nothing else to do with him. This life ain't mine anyway. It's his. I just wanted to get in where I fit in. But, if he would be that cruel, I don't and can't fit in with him or his crazy ass family," I said. I could tell Yaz and Tam were taken aback, but they knew me well enough to know that I was very serious. I didn't care if they still chose to talk to their men, but I would for sure be done with mine. In no time, we had all gotten in Tam's car and, together, we rode out to the Delgado estate for answers.

****

As we pulled up to Rah's house, there had been specific instructions for him to speak with me alone. So, Tam and Yaz put me out at his house and they drove a lil further down to Heavy's house. Before getting out, I told Tam to not get too comfortable because if this conversation didn't go as I hoped it would, I would be leaving immediately.

I was nervous but pissed at the same time. The man I had fallen in love with could've been the one responsible for what had happened to my brother. *How could he?* I asked myself as I walked into his house. Rah was sitting on the sectional with a drink in his hand and a concerned expression on his face.

"How's your brother?" he asked.

"Funny you should ask that Rah. I called to tell you what had happened and you never answered. So, how do you know about my brother?"

"Because Yaz told Smoke and he told me."

"Is that right?" I pondered in a serious tone.

"I think it's best if you sit down, so we can talk."

"Talk about what?" I asked as I walked closer to him. I couldn't hold it in any longer. "Rah, did you do this to my brother?"

He looked up at me with regretful eyes.

"What's that look about?"

"I don't even know where to begin," he said. "I've never been in a situation like this before."

"What did you do Rah? My brother is in a fucking coma!" I yelled before I knew it.

"Calm down," he said, still sitting down. I was sure he could see my frustrations in the matter. "I didn't do this to your brother."

"Well, if you didn't, who did?"

"I don't know," he responded. "I'm sure we have an idea though."

"What do you mean by that? Who is we?"

"Well, let me start me here. Last night when I dropped you off, I'd gotten a call telling me where your brother was at. Me, Heavy and Jose rode up on him. We followed him around for a bit and ended up in this alley."

"Omg, I don't know if I want to hear this," I mumbled with tears in my eyes. "You said you wouldn't hurt him."

"I didn't," Rah said. "Well, when we caught up with him, I just wanted to talk. I needed to know what he did with my shit. In that process, he was roughed up a bit but not by me."

"So, you're saying that you didn't do it but Heavy or Jose did? Like that's any better Rah! If they touched him, it was because of you. You control them."

Rah frowned. "I don't control my cousins. They do listen to me. However, your brother took a substantial amount of product from us. Did you actually expect us to be chill with that?"

"So, you do admit it. You did this to him."

"I didn't. We didn't," Rah said, with a shake of the head. "That's all you need to know."

"Oh, so it's like that?" I asked. "I couldn't believe that I was dealing with a man that would harm my brother. I don't care what he did.

"You wouldn't understand if I told you, so I'd rather not say. I will make this right, babe."

"How can you make this right? My brother is in a coma!" I cried out. "He could be dying as we speak!"

Rah stood up to try and console me, but I didn't want him touching me. Quickly, I pulled out my cell phone and called Tam.

"Please, come get me."

"Now?"

"Yes, NOW, Tam!" I yelled and ended the call. This shit was like a fucking nightmare that I wished I could wake up from. I just needed to get out of there and the quicker, the better.

****

One week turned into two and then week three rolled around even faster. My brother's condition still hadn't changed, and I was now doubting that it would. It was hard to face my parents day in and day out, sitting in that hospital watching them lose a piece of themselves as each day proved that my brother wasn't waking up. Somehow, I felt like I had all the answers to provide them but, then again, I didn't.

Tam was still seeing Heavy, as was Yaz still seeing Smoke. A part of me was in my feelings that they'd continue to see men that were from the Delgado family, especially Heavy, being that I knew he had something to do with my brother being in the condition he was in. Shit was crazy. I had basically fallen back from all of them. I was hurt and didn't know how to express that without snapping, so I'd been staying at my mom's house for the most part.

Now, I was sitting in my car outside of my condo with a different mindset of just wanting to make things right with my girls. During a time like this, I needed them the most. They didn't have nothing to do with CJ's attack, so why was I distancing myself from them? On top of that, they couldn't help who they loved. So, I unpacked that resentment and brought my butt back home.

The minute I entered the door, I smelled breakfast cooking. I smiled to myself, as Yaz called out.

"We're in the kitchen bitch!"

You just don't know how good that made me feel, as I headed in the kitchen. Immediately, I hugged Yaz and then Tam.

"I'm sorry I've been acting like an asshole."

"Girl, no need to apologize. We understand how you feel," Tam said.

"I knew you'd come around because we ain't did shit to you," Yaz teased. "But, seriously, we're hurting just like you are. Neither of us wanted this to happen to CJ, but what did he expect? He was the reason why your father's business almost went under. He took from his family, he took from Tam, he went in your closet and took some shit that definitely didn't belong to him so, in a sense, he took from you. I'm not saying that what happened to him was right, but you can't just keep fucking with people's shit and not expect nothing to happen to you."

"You're right," I said with a sense of truth coming over me. She was absolutely right. CJ had been taking from people for a long time. Unfortunately, for him, he'd barked up the wrong tree and was now stuck with nothing but prayers and high hopes that he'd make it down.

"On top of that, I know you're mad with Rah and Heavy but, from what Heavy told me, he only jacked your brother up and bitch slapped him in the face. Yes, he busted his lip, but that was it. He said that Rah stopped him and Jose from whooping his ass. When they left, CJ was okay. They never shot him or beat him to the degree that he'd been beaten. We just couldn't tell you that because you wasn't trying to hear nothing we had to say."

I stood there looking dumbfounded. "Is that mimosa for me?"

"Please, just take the whole champagne bottle. You need it," Yaz insisted, as she passed me the bottle. Without hesitation, I turned it up.

"So, have you talked to Rah?"

"No, I haven't. He called me for about a week and a half, but I wouldn't answer. Finally, he just stopped reaching out. If that's all that they did to my brother, then I totally feel like a piece of shit for treating him so cold. I have a feeling that he's probably over my ass by now and it's all my fault," I said, turning the bottle up again. "My life is in shambles right now and, I can't lie, I'm glad to be here with y'all. I've needed this for weeks."

"Yea, but your stubborn ass had kicked us to the curb," Tam joked. "Shit, I even thought you had moved out."

I grinned with a shake of the head. "It wasn't like that. I just didn't want to run into Heavy. I was definitely salty about my brother laying up in a hospital bed unconscious."

"I know girl, I was just playing," Tam said with a caring smile.

"I know," I said. "If only I had allowed Rah to explain fully, I would've known what really happened. He was just being so evasive and, even when I wouldn't answer, he didn't bother to text."

"You still haven't fully comprehended who you were fooling around with. Rah ain't used to this. Had it been somebody else's brother, he would've been a dead man the minute the shit happened. He held back because of you. He kept the dogs on a leash for as long as he could because of you. He didn't allow shit to go as bad as it could've because of you."

"I know and I feel bad as hell about it," I said, just as my cell phone began to ring. I looked at the display screen as my heart dropped.

"What?" Yaz asked.

"It's mama," I said, feeling scared to answer the phone.

"Answer it," Tam urged.

"Hey Ma," I answered. "Is everything okay?"

"Someone wants to speak with you."

"Who?" I asked, and the next voice I heard brightened my entire morning.

"Hey Sis."

"CJ!" I yelled out.

"Yes, the one and only," he teased in a groggy tone.

"Oh, my God, are you okay?"

"The doctor said that I will be. I just have to take it easy and allow myself to heal."

"When did you, I mean, what happened? I mean, when did you wake up?"

"Last night."

"Why didn't nobody call me? I wanted to be there."

"Dad felt it best to make sure that everything was straight first but, honestly, it feels like I've just been in a deep sleep and now I'm awake."

"Wow, this is a miracle and a blessing. We thought you weren't ever going to wake up."

"Well, it wasn't in God's plans," CJ said. "Look, I wanted to talk with you because I know I did some foul shit. Excuse my French," he said to mom and dad, "but can I have a minute alone to talk with Nova?"

Apparently, they did as he asked because a minute later, he resumed our conversation. "I've not been the best brother or son to you or mom and dad, and I'm sorry for that. This was really a wakeup call for me."

"You don't have to talk about this right now."

"But, I do," CJ said. "That night when this shit happened, I was approached by some men in an alley that I didn't know. It wasn't them that I was initially meeting there. However, I found out real fast who they were. I not only put myself in danger, but you could've been in danger too, from what I had done. That guy that you talk to though, loves you and I know that because he said it to me when he stopped his people from killing me. They left me there after I'd told them where their product was. Then, the goons I thought I had settled my debt with decided that they wanted to teach me an even bigger lesson. So, here I was thinking that we were meeting up so he could pay me for the extra product that he'd gotten from me. But, I was wrong. What I didn't know was that they wanted me completely out the picture, that way it would be no ties between us or that product that I'd stolen out of your closet. I wasn't thinking clearly because I should've known that something of that magnitude had to be coming from someone that was huge in the game. The only thing I was thinking about was saving my own ass because them niggas was out to get me. I'd crossed the wrong muthafuckas and they were ready for me to pay up or get laid down."

"So, somebody else did this to you? What if they find out you're still alive and come back to finish the job?"

"I made a phone call this morning and found out that they're dead now."

"Who's dead?"

"The man that I paid my debt to. Him and his

brother are dead."

"Wow," I said.

"I know right. From what I'm told, they were killed about a week after they did this to me."

"So, they won't be coming back?"

"No, and I hope nobody else will be coming back either. I'm done fucking over people. I just want to get it right this time. Fuck that, I love my life."

I grinned in the phone. "I know you do. I love your life too," I teased him.

"But look Sis. Mom just came back in with the doctor, so I'll call you later. Matter of fact, get your ass back up here so I can see you."

"You know I'm coming," I said with a big smile on my face. "I love you, Bro."

"Love you too," he said, and, with that, we ended our call.

"OMG!!" Tam let out. "He's okay!!"

"Yes, he's okay," I cheerfully expressed.

"Thank God!" Yaz chimed in. After we'd done our happy dance and I explained everything that CJ had told me, missing Rah hit me harder than ever.

"What's wrong?" Tam asked.

"I hate I treated Rah so bad, especially after hearing CJ said that Rah told him he loved me. I feel like somebody punched me in the gut."

"Don't feel that way. Just call him," Tam urged.

"NOW!" Yaz exclaimed. I pulled my phone out and called his phone. To my surprise, he sent me straight to voicemail.

"Damn y'all. He sent me to his voicemail," I sadly told them.

"Well, just chill out. He'll come around. I'm sure," Tam said.

"I just feel so bad. What if he don't come around? Lord, I need a sign or something. Please steer me in the right direction, so I can get my man back." At that time, the doorbell rang as Tam's eyes lit up.

"Shit, that might be him steering your ass. Go to the door."

I frowned as I shot her the side-eye. "Don't be playing with me."

"No, don't you be playing with God," she teased back, as I headed to the door.

"Who is it?" I asked, at the same time as opening the door. My eyes widened as a huge smile spread across my face. "Wow, you're here."

"Where else would I be?" Rah asked me with gentle eyes as he stared deeply in my soul. "Tam called and told me that you were coming here this morning, so I thought I'd surprise you by just showing up," he told me.

"Come here," I said, pulling him to me and hugging him tightly. "I missed you. I missed you so much."

"I missed you too," he said, kissing me on the lips. "I'm sorry about what happened, and I hope that your brother will be okay."

"He is okay. He woke up this morning."

"Oh, that is good news," Rah expressed. "That's great news."

I looked at him with sincere eyes, as he walked in further. "I just want to say thanks for all you've done. My brother told me what happened that night and I'm sorry I didn't hear you out."

"It's okay. I understood."

"No but really, I'm sorry. I won't ever do that again."

"It's okay," he assured me. "I love you and I want to be with you. I've not felt this way about a woman in a long time and I want to make sure that I don't ever lose you," he said, pulling out a bling of a nice ass ring.

"What the hell, babe?" I excitedly expressed.

"This is a promise ring," he told me. "I promise to never leave you astray. I promise to always love you no matter what. And I promise that someday you will be my wife. If you promise to just give me that chance, I want you to wear this ring."

With a smile so big that my jaws were hurting, I said, "I promise." Faintly, I could hear Yaz and Tam in the background cheering us on, but I was too consumed with the love that I was feeling as Rah passionately kissed me. Now, I could enjoy the endless possibilities of a happily ever after with the man of my dreams.

The End...

Other Books Written by Tiece...

*Rich Boy Thuggin' Is A Whole Vibe (A Complete Novel)

*Falling In Love With The Goat 1-3 (Complete Series) Also available in a 3 book Box Set.

*Just Can't Leave Him Alone 1-5, Originally Titled, CheckMate (Complete Series)

*I Need Love 1-4, Originally Titled, SCARLETT (Complete Series)

*Drunk in Love 1-4 (Also Available In a Complete Box-set)

*Woman To Woman 1-3 (Also Available in a Complete box-set)

*The First Wife 1-3 (Part 4 still in the works) *Shanice Capone's Truth, A Shorty Story (Located at the end of The First Wife part 3)

*Classy & Ratchet, Originally Titled, Ratchet Bitches 1-2

*Southern Gossip 1-2
*It's Either Me Or Her 1-2

*A Boss Valentine In Atlanta
(A Short Story)
*These Games We Play
*Dopeboyz & the Women That Love 'em

CPSIA information can be obtained
at www.ICGtesting.com
Printed in the USA
LVHW031613171220
674449LV00002B/380